Renewed by Grace

Book Four of the Grace Series

Anna Christine Boulier

First published by Anna Christine Boulier in 2019
Copyright © Anna Christine Boulier, 2019
All rights reserved. No part of this publication may be reproduced, stored or transmitted in any form or by any means, electronic, mechanical, photocopying, recording, scanning, or otherwise without written permission from the publisher. It is illegal to copy this book, post it to a website, or distribute it by any other means without permission.

This novel is a work of fiction. Names, characters, and incidents are either the product of the author's imagination or are used fictitiously, and any resemblance to actual persons, living or dead, events or localities is entirely coincidental.

For permission contact:
www.acboulier.com
writer@acboulier.com

Cover Design By: Anna Christine Boulier
First edition

The Grace Series

Restoring Grace
Book One in the Grace Series

Accepting Grace
Book Two in the Grace Series

Trusting Grace
Book Three in the Grace Series

Renewed by Grace
Book Four in the Grace Series

Healing Grace
Book Five in the Grace Series
Coming August 2019

*This book is dedicated to
Michelle Morton and Inga Williams.*

I can never thank you both enough for taking a chance on me – I wouldn't be where I am at today if you two had not seen potential in me even I wasn't aware of.

Thank you for being two of the best managers I've ever had and teaching me how to be the best version of me.

He saved us, not because of works done by us in righteousness, but according to his own mercy, by the washing of regeneration and RENEWAL of the Holy Spirit.

—Titus 3:5 ESV

ACKNOWLEDGEMENT

Thank you to my editors Anne Boulier and Erin Boulier who spent a few of their evenings listening to me read through the novel.

Thank you to my wonderful Beta Readers- both the new and tried and true: Diane Gaseway, Lisa LeMasters, Blair St. John, Helene Horgan, and Bea Beville.

Prologue

March 1990

"Mom, please read another chapter. Pleeease?"

Andrea looked into her son's green eyes and could see they were still red from crying earlier in the evening after James fussed at him to quit practicing the trumpet. He had yelled the noise was giving him a raging headache and then stormed out of the living room.

"It's late, Joshua. You have school tomorrow."

Joshua leaned forward, his eyes shining. "I know, but Skip's in danger of being captured!"

Tousling his hair, Andrea smiled to see her serious little man acting like the five-year-old he really was. "Okay, but only one more chapter... no matter what happens. Deal?" She gave him her mother stare as she said, "You've got that big sight word test tomorrow."

"Deal!" Joshua laid back down, snuggling under the sheets covered in spaceships and planets. "I like numbers more, but I don't really have to study."

Rolling her eyes, Andrea picked up the book again. "Don't tell me that!"

Shifting on the side of the bed, she opened the latest Kip novel to the next chapter and began to read out loud. "Kip struggled to unlock the bulkhead door, muttering under his breath Neptune should be here. 'What's the point of having a genius talking dog if he isn't around to help you...'"

As Andrea continued the next chapter in the Skip Saturn series, she wondered if the baby she was carrying would be good for both Joshua and James. Rubbing her still flat stomach, she thought, *it'll be nice for Joshua to have a constant friend since we move around so much with James' job in the military. I was going to tell James at dinner tonight, but it will have to wait until tomorrow.*

After Kip had escaped once again, Andrea tucked her little man in for the night.

"Goodnight, son. Sleep well and say your prayers."

"Night, Mom. You'll read again to me tomorrow night, too, won't you?" His eyes were shining in expectation of further adventures.

"Yes, my little astronaut."

Turning off the light, she watched Joshua settle in and made sure the Superman nightlight was on, before making her way to her bedroom. Right before dinner, James had gotten a call that sent him rushing over to base headquarters for an emergency, and she didn't expect to see him that night. She put her robe at the foot of the bed in case Joshua called out for her and climbed under the covers. Andrea reached into the drawer of her nightstand and grabbed a paperback novel she had shoved all the way to the back. She opened up to the last page she had read and muttered, "I have to be up early too and can only read one chapter myself. After I drop Joshua off at school, I've got that committee meeting to plan the annual Marine Corp gala. If I'd known I'd be pregnant during the event, I wouldn't have volunteered to head up the entire thing."

Two hours later, the novel almost finished having read five chapters, Andrea closed the book and put it in the back of her nightstand drawer. *Oh, Lord, it's after eleven. I can't believe I stayed up so late reading Mark Lawson's latest sci-fi novel!?! Who would've thought how much I'd enjoy the adult series of Kip Saturn. No one would believe I've loved reading science fiction since I was a teenager, but something about the man's writing makes me think I'm watching a movie, not just reading a book.* Taking a sip of water, she paused placing it on the nightstand. *I've read two novels in this series, but something's different about this one. I'm struggling to put it down.*

Not surprised James wasn't back, Andrea turned off the lights and snuggled under the covers. *Lord, please let this baby be good for our family. James and I discussed not having another child right now, because he's going on tour in a few weeks...*

Sighing, Andrea turned over to grab his pillow to smell his aftershave. *Lord, I trust You have a plan for this unexpected blessing. Help me to follow the path You have for our family. Amen.*

Feeling at peace, Andrea fell asleep with his aftershave filling her senses. When James got home right before dawn, he smiled to see his wife holding his pillow, and gently moved her closer to his side to wrap his arms around her. Falling asleep was always better with Andrea in his arms and with only a short time until he had to be back on base and then gone away on another tour, he wanted all the time with her he could get.

Mark's Journal Entry - March 28, 1990

Lord,

I'm not the best at talking and I'm new to this praying thing, so I thought I'd write out my thoughts in this journal Maggie gave me for Christmas. Last week, she gave me a chance to have Christmas with Kip under her and Rick's supervision, because she said she had seen a real change since January after I was saved. I truly believe it was a miracle after everything I've done. I know it's only because of You my ex-wife is giving me a second chance with my son. Thank You for this unexpected second chance!

I'll try to always be honest in these journal entries and consistent, too. If I can write on my novels most every day, then well, I can write to You as well.

My editor contacted me this afternoon and said my writing must have greatly improved because the publishing house is getting a lot of positive feedback from my novel that launched last week. David was astonished when I gave him the newest Kip novel months ahead of schedule. I don't know what happened, but after I was saved in January, I had all this energy. I went to my room and wrote everything out. It's never come so easily before, and I know it was because of You, too.

Please help me to be not just a better writer, but a Christian author who needs to be held to a higher standard. People reading my books should be led to You, not away from You. Help me to be the man of God You want me to be.

I want my son to be proud of his father, and I know it means I've got to keep walking the walk of faith. Please help me not to disappoint my family.

Chapter One

September 2013

"Come on Andrea! Just four more and you're done."

Andrea lifted her eyes, sweat shimmering on her forehead. Trying not to glare at her physical therapist, she muttered, "I'm tired, Matt, and this was a looong session for this fifty-year-old lady."

"Yes, but it's your last one." Matt looked at the petite older woman and marveled at her energy even after the few complaints she'd made during physical therapy.

"You can do it, Mrs. Andrea. I'll do four more if you will."

Andrea looked over at the young boy who spoke and smiled. *Lord, thank You for sending this sweet boy to encourage me through this painful process. I couldn't have made it through without him.*

"Ok, Noah. Just for you, I'll do four more!" Winking at the blond-haired, blue-eyed boy, she struggled through her last few exercises, before collapsing in a chair. "I thought with this being my last session, you would've taken it easy on me!"

"I can't help how well you're doing, Andrea. You've been a great patient. You've done beautifully and could probably run a 5K." Matt handed Andrea a towel, before giving Noah a high five. "Good job, Noah!"

Kristy, Noah's physical therapist said to the boy, "You're done for the day, Mr. Noah. I'll see you next week." Noah giggled at the young woman calling him mister and gave her a high five before grabbing his bookbag. Kristy called to the back of his head, "And don't forget your exercises."

Matt hugged Andrea, before he said, "Keep up with your exercises too, and remember to be mindful of your hip." Making notes on her chart, he continued, "Your body will tell you when you need to slow down. Be sure to walk every day."

"Thank you, Matt. You've been great." Pushing her curly brown hair out of her face, she smiled throwing him the soggy towel. "I wouldn't be back to normal so quickly without your help."

"You did the work. I just showed you what to do."

Noah waited by the door for Andrea to get her purse before following her outside to sit on the bench. It was still warm for September, and Noah liked being able to spend so much time outside. *When we lived in Chicago, it was usually freezing by now.*

Andrea sat down next to Noah and sighed. "I'm going to miss seeing you two times a week, Noah. You've been such an encouragement to this old woman."

Noah smiled while shaking his head, "You're not old, plus you're fun. I like all your stories."

"You're just easy to talk to and I do love talking about my boys."

"I want to meet Josh and Jacob someday. They sound like fun. I've always wanted a pet frog, but Mom says no pets until I'm older."

"I'd love for you to meet my sons. I think they'd like you, too." Andrea hugged the little boy, before looking away. *I haven't seen Jacob in so long, I don't know if I'd even recognize him.*

Shaking her head over the sad thought, she changed the subject by asking, "Is your Grandpa picking you up today?"

Noah nodded, "Yeah, he's been writing all morning, but will pick me up this afternoon since my parents are working."

"It's good he can do that."

Looking out for cars, she was hoping to finally meet the grandpa Noah raved about day after day. All she really knew was he was trying to write a science fiction story based on Noah and the little boy was excited to have books written specifically about him. *It was talking about science fiction that allowed us to bond. Noah was shocked to learn this fifty-year-old woman knew so much about sci-fi.*

Glancing sideways at the smiling boy, she thought, *I'm not sure what the publishing world looks like, but I hope the boy knows it will probably be small. I imagine it's hard to get into the traditional publisher's market.* Glancing at Noah, she sighed, *But, I'm sure he'll be happy with whatever his grandfather does. I've never seen a boy adore his grandfather more than Noah does.*

"Mrs. Andrea?"

"Yes, Noah?"

"Will you come to my birthday party?"

Andrea's smile went from ear to ear. "Of course, honey! I wouldn't miss it. When is it?"

Before Noah could reply, Andrea's phone rang. She mouthed to Noah, "just a sec" and then said, "Hello, Bailey!" She paused before asking, "What did Josh do now?"

Noah watched her on the phone and prayed his grandfather would arrive soon. He had been trying to get them to meet since Mrs. Andrea started physical therapy with him in July. Now it was September, and he was out of time. *Today's her last day! Come on, Grandpa. You can't miss meeting her this time. It's the last chance we've got.*

"Noah, that was Bailey. I've told you about her running the catering part of Taste & See with me. I need to go, we're catering an event for the youth silent auction tomorrow and I've got to grab a few things my son forgot. Apparently, he went to the grocery store to buy baking powder and brought home baking soda instead. Bailey's practically in tears. I need to get the shopping done quickly and get home before they kill each other."

Noah laughed, but only thought, *that sounds like my dad, he forgets stuff all the time.* Standing up, Andrea hugged Noah. "You'll be okay waiting for your Grandpa?"

The little boy nodded, unable to hide his frown, "Bye, Mrs. Andrea."

Watching her walk away, Noah groaned. *How will I get her to meet Grandpa, now?* As she drove away, he waved goodbye. *Oh, no!* He slapped his forehead as her car pulled out of the parking lot. *I forgot to tell her my birthday!*

Moments later, a dark jeep pulled in front of Noah and honked. The little boy hopped off the bench to wave at his grandpa. "Grandpa, you're late!" He said with his hands on his skinny hips.

"I know, bud, but there was a bad accident on the highway and I was stuck." Mark was surprised to see his grandson so upset. *Noah's usually very go with the flow, easy going.*

"I wanted you to meet my friend Andrea, but she left already."

"Sorry, bud. Next time." *This upset over a girl, that's new!*

Noah hung his head, "This was her last day of therapy."

"Ohh!" Understanding dawned on him that his grandson's crush wasn't going to be there anymore. *Poor guy, no wonder he's sad.* Mark wanted to cheer him up asked, "Well, won't you see her at school?"

"GRANDPAAAA! I told you she DOESN'T go to my school."

"Umm!" Mark put the jeep in gear. "Well, we'll think of something. I mean would Kip Saturn let his friend go off to another planet without ever seeing her again."

The little boy's eyes shined bright. "No, he would have his faithful Neptune track her down."

"Exactly!"

"I invited her to my birthday party, but I don't have her address to mail her an invitation." He tossed his backpack in the floor of the jeep, "I didn't get to tell her when it is or it's about space."

"Well, I'm sure we can track it down. We've got time, your birthday's not until mid-December." Turning onto the highway, Mark asked, "Milkshake before we go home and you do your homework?"

Fist pump into the air, Noah shouted, "YES!"

Mark turned toward their favorite ice cream place and wondered about the child named Andrea, who had his grandson so mesmerized. *He's never had a crush on a girl before, always saying they had cooties. I may be fifty-three, but I remember girls and cooties. I guess this means my little guy is really growing up.* Listening to Noah sing along to the praise and worship CD he had playing, Mark sighed, *oh to be young and in love.*

Chapter Two

"Andrea, would you hand me another one of Bailey's muffins? They're so good."

Andrea stood to grab the box from the table laden with goodies and smiled while passing them to Laura. "They're really yummy. Bailey made them for Josh. They were his favorite growing up."

"I can taste the peanut butter, but what else did she put in these things?"

"Honey."

Nodding, Laura took another bite. Trying not to frown, Andrea wondered for the twentieth time that morning what was going on between her business partner and oldest son. They had been dating since July and everything was fine until Viviane and Cole's wedding in September. Now the first Thursday in October, it looked like Bailey and Josh had an awful fight and weren't speaking to each other. *I feel so helpless, Lord.*

Staring out the window in the fellowship hall at church, Andrea thought to herself, *I still don't even know what happened. Bailey said she doesn't want to put me in the middle, but I've seen her red-rimmed eyes too much for my liking. I have a feeling Josh did something stupid. He can be so stubborn sometimes.*

"Andrea? Andrea? Are you listening?"

Shaking her head, Andrea turned to one of the ladies speaking to her. "Sorry, Betty. I was thinking about something." Forcing herself to focus on the plump matron in her seventies, Andrea prepared herself for something wild. *Betty Lu Richardson never does anything halfway and she's been unusually quiet for this month's widow's meeting.*

"I said I need to ask you a question." Pursing her red lips, she cocked her head so her large gold earrings clinked, a serious look on her face, she said, "I wanted to know if you think two years is long enough to wait before I start dating again?"

Andrea choked on the sweet tea she was drinking and tried to hide her shock. *The woman's in her seventies and wants to start dating?!? Oh, Lord!*

"Betty Lu Richardson are you out of your mind?" Beverly, another member at Great Hills Christian church cried out, causing the rest of the group of women to turn toward their end of the table.

"Well, I'm NOT getting any younger." Betty slapped her hand on the table, causing her drink glass to shake. "And that nice Dr. Kline has been flirting with me for over a month now."

Clearing her throat, Andrea asked, "Dr. Kline?" Frowning, she continued, "Dr. Kline, the retired doctor who tries to diagnosis everyone with some terrible ailment?" She pictured the older gentleman, balding and usually in suits too big for him with brightly colored bow-ties.

Nodding her head, Betty's earrings jangled loudly. "Yes, he's been flirting with me for weeks now before church service. I think he wants to ask me out and I think... well... I think I want to say yes." Frowning, she said, "Up until now, I always changed the subject when he starts asking me about my plans for Friday night." Looking at Andrea, while nervously shredding her napkin, she asked, "Do you think, it's too soon?"

"Well..." Andrea paused. *Lord, why is she asking me? I can see she's upset, she's so worried over it which isn't like her.*

Beverly piped up, "If you have the energy and so does, Dr. Kline, I say go for it." Looking at Andrea and Laura sitting beside each other, Beverly pointed at them, "It would be good if others in this group would start dating, too!"

Laura slouched down in her chair, but Andrea gave a half shrug. "I'm too set in my ways. I like going where I want and doing what I like."

"Don't you get lonely?" Betty asked, everyone focusing on Andrea waiting for her reply.

"No," Andrea frowned. *Do I, Lord? When Bailey and Josh were dating, I did have more free time, especially since Bailey became a partner in the catering business and everything doesn't rest all on my shoulders... but I'm still busy and active... it's just at night sometimes...* Shaking her head, she thought, *But now I'm staying in the little mother-in-law suite off the main house, I don't feel lonely rattling around in that big house in the evenings... Right?*

One of the other ladies piped up, interrupting her thoughts. "It's not for everyone to date again. I mean, look at Delia Anne, she's been a widow for over thirty years."

Another lady in the group, who had been widowed for a few years called out, "That's true, it isn't for everyone. I wouldn't want to be married again either."

As the ladies debated dating or not, Andrea watched Laura quietly stand and begin to clean the food table from their lunch meeting. Looking at her watch, Andrea saw it was almost two, but thought it was a bit early for Laura to start packing up. *She must be upset. She's never talked about dating again, and the young widow's only twenty-seven years old.*

Walking over, Andrea helped Laura begin to clean the dishes. Whispering quietly, Andrea asked, "Are you okay, Laura?"

Laura looked up with a half-smile, her blue-gray eyes sad. "Yes, I just didn't have anything to contribute to the conversation and I know our meeting will be over soon."

Andrea only nodded putting lids on containers. "It's okay if you don't want to date. Age shouldn't have anything to do with dating."

"Thanks," Laura paused to quickly to wipe away a tear. "I've never really talked about it, but my marriage with Blake wasn't the best. I'm not sure if I ever want to be married again. I don't know if I can go through that a second time."

Sending up a prayer for the hurting young woman, Andrea reached out to squeeze her hand. "If you ever need to talk, just you and me, please feel free to call me." *I guessed as much from the way she's reacted around men when we've gone out to lunch together. I always thought her husband might've been abusive, but she's never wanted to talk about it.*

"Thank you, Andrea. I'm not quite at a place where I can talk about it." Sighing, she admitted, "Even though it HAS been two years already." Placing a lid on a plastic container, she moved a bit closer to whisper, "Blake's family wants to move here to see more of their grandson. They've been visiting almost every weekend to look at houses. I'm too stressed right now to deal with much of anything."

"Your mother mentioned your in-laws at the silent auction last month."

"Yes, she's angry I won't stand up to them, but they lost their only son and my son, Brian, is the only grandchild they have."

"That sounds like a hard place to be in."

Laura nodded, "It is." With a sigh, she continued, "I'm praying for God to show me what to do. They've looked at so many houses, I don't know if they'll ever pick one. I can't keep having them at my place all weekend... I have a guestroom, but it's hard having so many people in my little three-bedroom apartment. I'd been looking for a house, but we moved back to Cartersville so quickly after Blake's death. Well...I took what I could find fast, but I really want Brian to have a home with a yard."

"You poor thing." Hugging Laura, Andrea sent up another prayer. "I'll be praying God works out this whole situation."

"Thank you."

"Andrea?"

Turning around, Andrea saw Betty walking up to her, only a little taller than Andrea's own five-foot height in heels. Stopping in front of the two ladies, Betty looked at her with a large grin on her face. "I've decided I'm going to let dear Dr. Kline ask me out this Sunday."

"Well, that sounds like a good idea," Andrea said handing the woman her empty dish.

Betty took the plate and smiled at both Laura and Andrea. "Thank you for your input, because I value your opinion. Since you started this widow's group at the church, I've felt more connected to people... less lonely. I look forward to the first Thursday of each month." Bobbing her head sent her earrings clinking, "I'll see you Sunday."

With a quick wave goodbye, the feisty woman marched out already planning on buying a new outfit for this Sunday. Andrea watched her go and wondered if she would ever consider dating again. She snorted, *Maybe I'll just get a dog instead. I could go to the humane society and get an older dog who would have a harder time finding a home. It would help me to continue walking more like my physical therapist wanted and keep me company at the same time.*

Pleased with her decision, Andrea finished cleaning up and waved goodbye to the ladies as they left. When it was only her and Laura, Andrea reminded her, "Don't forget to call me if you need anything, even if all you need to do is vent to someone. I'm happy to listen."

She smiled looking out the window. "I never told anyone this, but shortly after I married James, I really struggled to get along with his mother." She leaned against the table, "That woman was positively hateful to me, especially when James was on tour. She and James's father were divorced and she took her hurt and anger out on me."

Andrea remembered it as if it were only yesterday. "One day at church, I met this sweet woman who saw me break down in the bathroom because I was so overwhelmed having to meet her for dinner later that night. She held me while I cried and let me vent to her when I needed it... it marked a change in my life. I KNOW God sent her to me when I needed someone."

Tears in her eyes, Laura hugged her. "I'm glad God put you in my life. I've never talked to anyone about Blake, not even my parents. I think they had suspicions, but I lived far away when I was married, only moving back after Blake died..."

Laura leaned back, sighing, "I do need to talk to someone, but I've got to get Brian from school." She paused, hesitating, "Could... could we do lunch next week sometime? I'm going to need to start talking about things or I know I'm going to blow up sometime when Blake's parents are here." Sighing, Laura muttered, "They remind me of him in some ways with their violent outbursts and arguing."

"Of course."

Smiling, the ladies made their way out with one last hug. Andrea prayed for Laura as she drove off. *Lord, please help me to be a friend to her. I don't know why she pulls at my heartstrings, but she does. I can't ever understand what she's been through, but I do want to help her in any way I can.*

Turning toward the outskirts of town, Andrea decided not to drive straight home but drove to the Etowah Humane Society. *I think it's time I find myself a dog.*

Anna Christine Boulier

Mark's Journal Entry - October 3, 2013

Lord,

I had a really good writing day today. I've been going all around Cartersville and surrounding areas to find places to write when I'm stuck or can't seem to settle down to work at home. I'm glad I followed Kip and Becka down to this little, but fast-growing town. Now I'm settled in this tiny rental house, I feel like I'm where I'm supposed to be. I know my son and his wife, Becka, like having me near to help with the kids because of their crazy work hours. Being a doctor and children's counselor, they have hectic schedules and need the flexibility I bring with my open schedule. Plus, I enjoy seeing Noah and Eva every day and being able to watch them grow up.

Noah reminds me so much of Kip at that age. His birthday's in December and he'll turn eight. When Kip turned eight, I was already divorced from his mom and she had severely limited my contact, not letting me see him alone. I was furious back then, angry she took my son away and wouldn't let me see him when I wanted. Angry my own father was gone and I couldn't resolve anything... angry at myself for becoming just like my old man.

Maggie was right to keep Kip away from me, and things worked out for the best. She's happily married to Rick, and he's been a great stepfather to my boy. I consider their daughter April, my niece and she even calls me, Uncle Mark.

Being honest with myself, right now, I feel restless in a way I've never felt before. It's strange how I'm content with things, but still, wonder about more... maybe I just need to focus on the new book series based on Noah's name. I'm probably just mixed up about that, since I've been writing Kip Saturn stories for most of my adult life. I'm sure that's it!

I know Noah's birthday is coming up and he's begging me almost daily to find a way to get an invitation to his little friend, Andrea. Lord, I could use Your help with this one, because I don't know how to track down a child without looking like a dirty old man. Help me, please.

Chapter Three

"Come in, Grace. Hi, Bailey."

Andrea held the door open wide and enjoyed the confused look on Bailey's face. *Lord, please let tonight go well for both Josh and Bailey. I've been praying for two days this all works out according to Your plan.*

"What's going on? Grace said you called and needed me to check something out?" Bailey put her purse down on the little table in the entryway and then stood with her hands on her hips. Frowning at both her best friend, Grace, and Andrea, her business partner, Bailey tapped her foot waiting for an answer. *They're up to something, I know it! I can always tell when Grace has a secret, and it's written all over her face.* Glancing at Andrea, she fumed, *Now that I see Andrea's smirk, I know they're in this together!*

"Bailey, you know with the mother-in-law suite done, Michael Adams will be starting on the barn and..."

"Andrea," Bailey huffed, "We've talked about what needed to be done to the barn months ago! I know Michael's going to start working on the barn soon, but he wanted to get the foundation laid for the indoor building we're adding before the weather got bad."

"I know dear," Andrea smiled innocently, "But, I want to make sure our plans are still good for the barn. After all, we're partners and we both need to have a say."

"We've discussed this same subject dozens of times. There are even a few pages in one of your notebooks outlining everything we wanted to fix up in a nice, neat list." Closing her eyes, Bailey quoted from memory, "New windows, plank flooring so no one's shoes are messed up, a side room added for storage so we don't have to lug furniture back and forth between the new structure and the barn..."

"I know Bales, but Michael starts Monday and I want to make sure you're sure."

Raising her eyebrow, Bailey mumbled "fine" and started walking out to the large barn. Turning she saw Andrea and Grace watching her from the window. "Aren't you two coming?"

Nodding their heads, no, Andrea yelled back, "I don't have the right shoes on. Don't worry. You'll be fine."

"Yes, Bales. It'll be fine. We love you."

As Bailey stomped off in her three-inch heels she muttered, "Crazy women! Talk about inappropriate footwear, I'M in inappropriate footwear. I never wear heels! These are actually Grace's shoes. She absolutely INSISTED I borrow them tonight. The pair of flats I had on were perfectly fine, but NOOO..."

Andrea and Grace watched her stomp around the corner to the barn entrance and knew immediately when she saw Josh as her hand flew to her mouth and she cut her eyes back at them for a moment.

Andrea grinned, *I know it would be rude to watch their date, but oh how I wish I could be a fly on the wall.*

Grace must have been thinking the same thing, laughing, "It's a good thing I know Bales will tell me every detail about tonight, or else I'd be outside looking through one of the windows."

Andrea chuckled, "I know what you mean. Would you like some sweet tea while we wait?"

Grace turned with a grin. "Yes, please."

While Andrea went to pour a drink, Grace sat at the island to talk. "I'm glad Josh and the gang came up with this big plan to win Bailey back. Even though I was mad at him for hurting her, they're perfect for each other."

Andrea snorted, "Yes, and thankfully Bailey's kindhearted, she'll forgive the oaf. Josh has good friends to help him out. I'm glad everyone let me in on the plan Thursday afternoon. It's been hard the past few weeks not knowing what happened. I was going crazy wondering and neither one of them would share."

Before Grace could respond, Viviane came running in from the barn. "I've got to start getting the food ready. Cole will be here in a few minutes to take it out to them."

Grace jumped up to help and the women quickly got a fancy meal put together. Viviane had just placed the small vase with flowers on the tray when Cole walked in the kitchen side door. Seeing him, Grace began to giggle at him wearing a black tuxedo with a towel draped over his arm, but she doubled over laughing when he started speaking in a horrible French accent. "Pardon, ladies. I must hurry back to the lovebirds."

"You went all out, Cole," Grace waved at his outfit. "You guys have thought of everything."

"You should have heard him this week practicing that awful French accent. He's already driving me crazy and we haven't even been married a month." Viviane grinned at Cole, giving him a wink as he backed out the door with the tray of food.

"Ignore my wife, she's madly in love with me. True amore and all that." Cole cried out in his French accent before he carried Josh and Bailey's dinner out to the barn.

The three women laughed at Cole's antics as Andrea placed a glass of tea in front of both Grace and Viviane.

After saying thank you, Viviane asked, "So what have you been up to? I haven't seen you since we got back from our honeymoon."

Taking a deep breath, Andrea said quickly, "I'm getting a dog."

"Oh, that's wonderful. What kind, when?" Viviane asked.

"A sweet beagle mix. When I saw her, I just knew she was the one. She looked like she was covered in blueberry spots in the kennel's light, so I'm calling her Muffin. Blueberry muffins have always been my favorite."

"How sweet! Did you find her at the Etowah Humane Society?" Grace asked sipping on her tea.

"Yes, I'll pick her up tomorrow afternoon. She's around five years old and was dumped one morning a few months ago."

"Oh, that's awful." Grace set down her glass.

"Yes, she had never been spayed, but she'll be ready to come home with me tomorrow. The doctor just wanted to check her out once more before I bring her home since she was older dog. They don't adopt out pets that aren't fixed. I spent this afternoon buying dog supplies. I spent a small fortune, but couldn't help myself once I got started."

She stopped talking a moment and went to grab some of the things she bought, showing off the piles of stuff. After she had shown Grace and Viviane everything, she paused a moment, hesitating in turning to Grace, "She's a sweet little dog and the lady said she'd be good to have around because she stays really calm. I don't know how Bailey would feel with a dog around the house, especially when she's cooking..."

"Don't worry. Bales loves animals, having spent her summers on her grandmother's ranch. Her lifestyle at the restaurant didn't allow her to have a pet, but she's been wondering about getting a dog now she's settled in Cartersville and her work hours aren't so extensive."

"Oh, good!" Andrea's hand rising to her chest, "That was the only thing I was really worried about.

"Is that music?"

Nodding, Andrea said, "They must be done eating and are dancing now."

"OHH! I don't want to miss this. Do you think we could we go watch?" Viviane asked already rising to her feet.

"Yes, let's go. I've been patient long enough!" Grace said with a giggle.

"I'm standing in the front," Andrea insisted, tossing a towel on the counter.

The three ladies walked quietly out to the barn to find Cole already looking through one of the cracked windows. All four of them crowded around to watch Bailey and Josh dance slowly around the dance floor the group had set up only hours earlier. Cole and Viviane watched arm in arm, while Andrea felt blessed she and Josh had moved to this lovely town.

All these unexpected blessings, Lord. You knew Bailey would be here... they would fall in love... I'm so glad I got to see this. Thinking about Betty Lu wanting to date, Andrea wondered a moment if she should think about dating... *After all, I'll only be fifty-one in December. That's not old.* She shook her head, *But I'm like Delia Anne, set in my ways.*

"Aren't they a sweet couple?" Grace whispered to Andrea.

Andrea only nodded, *I never dreamed they'd fall in love. It never crossed my mind with how they first reacted to each other.* Sighing, Andrea thanked God for sending Bailey into their lives.

It seemed like the group had been spying for a long time because it had gotten dark outside. They were considering walking away when they watched Josh pull out a small jewelry box.

Viviane gasped, "Andrea? Did you know?" The young woman started jumping up and down. "Oh, he's going to propose! I pray she says yes."

"I suspected. He asked for my mother's engagement ring yesterday. He knew it would go to him as the oldest son." Andrea wiped a tear from her eye, *Bailey will be my daughter officially now. There will be no in-laws for us.*

When Josh got on one knee, they watched Bailey stoop down to him and after a moment, they were kissing as Josh put the ring on her finger. The small group of friends couldn't keep quiet any longer and began shouting. Andrea saw Bailey look over and smile. She could see the contentment and happiness in Bailey's green eyes, even through the grimy windows.

When Josh turned toward them, everyone went rushing inside with congratulations. Andrea walked up to Bailey and hugged her tight. "Welcome to the family, my daughter."

"Thank you, Andrea. I love your son, and I have always loved and cared for you. I couldn't be happier if I tried." Bailey whispered in Andrea's ear, "Can I call you Mom, now? Not just a friend and business partner?"

Andrea stepped back with tears in her eyes, unable to stop the flow. She nodded as she strangled out, "Of course, welcome to the family, Bailey."

Chapter Four

"Muffin, the girls will be here in a few minutes and I need to change. Our walk took longer than I thought."

Rushing to her little mother-in-law suite off the main house, Andrea began changing from her workout clothes into jeans and a sweater. She laughed softly to see her dog follow her like Mary's little lamb. Muffin had been a blessing in the short week she had her. They had been walking around the property almost daily while the weather was still nice. She enjoyed seeing the progress Michael was making each day on the large new building that would be ready next spring for Taste & See to host large events on site.

It was getting cooler in the evenings, but she was surprised by how much she was enjoying the daily walks. She split her time talking to Muffin and the Lord, praying for direction about the future now Bailey was officially joining the family.

Hearing noise coming from the catering kitchen, she finished dressing quickly. Muffin barked and ran out to see who had come to play with her. Andrea walked back through the house to find Josh and Bailey putting Chinese food out for everyone coming over to help plan their wedding which was in a few weeks.

"Hey, Mom. How was your walk?"

"Good, Josh. I'm glad you two are here. I wanted to talk to both of you before everyone arrives."

"Oh?" Bailey asked, "Is something wrong?"

Andrea waved her hands, blurting out, "No. I wanted to know if you guys had thought about where you're going to live once you're married."

Josh and Bailey looked at each other, unsure what to say. They both knew Josh's apartment over the carriage house was too small for the two of them. "Josh could always move into my rental house. It's pretty close to here…"

Andrea snorted, "Loves of my life… why don't you move into this house? The upstairs master suite needs a new makeover and it does have the kitchen you work in most every day, Bales…"

"But Mom, this is your home! I know because of the car accident in June you decided to live in the cottage…" Josh walked over to put his arm around her. "It wouldn't be right and…"

"Josh," Andrea interrupted him, "I live almost entirely in the new addition. It has a large bed and bath, a small kitchen and living area. It's a little house all on its own and all I really need. There's no reason the two of you can't make the rest of this house yours. This is where our catering business is and unless you don't want me on the property…"

Before Andrea could continue, Bailey rushed over to put her arms around her future mother-in-law, "Don't ever think we don't want you here. I'd love to live in this house. It would make everything easier to work in the catering kitchen and besides, I've always loved this place. It feels like home."

Josh put his arms around his two favorite girls. "Then it's settled. I think this is the best thing that could happen. Thank you, Mom. You're the greatest."

"It just seemed like the best option for everyone."

"Yes, I just hate to have to leave my little rental house." Bailey moved to grab silverware. "I know the Adams had a hard time finding someone to rent it before I came along."

Andrea's eyes twinkled. "Don't worry, dear. I have a plan for your old place, too! But first, we need to get everything ready for everyone coming over. We've got a wedding to plan, and you've given us less than two months."

Bailey laughed, "Well, I wanted simple and quick after the months of planning the wedding with Preston's mother. After a broken engagement, I've waited long enough for the right guy to ask me and I'm not going to give him a chance to change his mind."

Josh leaned over and kissed her. "Never going to happen."

Andrea sighed and decided December seventh couldn't come fast enough to make Bailey officially a part of the family. "Well, we have the date and the location. I know the two of you wrote out the guest list this morning."

Sneaking an egg roll, Josh agreed, "Yes, Bailey and I discussed the big stuff earlier. While you ladies plan the nitty-gritty details, I'm going to get some work done. I told my bosses I don't want to travel much anymore. They're graciously transitioning me to a senior level position which oversees a team that travels, but I've got to get all my files organized for the guy taking over my old job."

Bailey laughed, "I guess I didn't believe he was a big deal at his work until they gave him a raise to keep him from leaving the company." Turning to Andrea, Bailey winked, "I fell in love with a brilliant man, Andrea Cabot."

Andrea groaned, "Bales, you're going to make his ego even bigger."

"Not possible," Bailey said with a grin. Fixing Josh his own plate, she kissed him before shooing him away. "It's girl time. I'll see you before I leave."

"Only forty-nine days until you can't get rid of me," He gave her a quick peck before he left for his carriage apartment carrying a tray of food.

Waiting until he was out of earshot, Andrea said, "As my wedding gift to you and Josh, I want to pay for the master suite makeover. Monday, let's go shopping and see what you'd like to do."

"You don't have to..."

"I know, but I want to."

Bailey was truly touched and wondered why her own mother couldn't love her like this woman had come to in such a short amount of time. "I tried calling my parents several times this week to tell them about my engagement, but they haven't answered. I didn't want to leave a message about something this important, but I might have to if they don't pick up soon."

She hugged the young woman who was trying to hide her tears, "I'm still praying for them."

"Thanks, Mom. It means a lot to me."

Before Bailey could say anymore Muffin barked and then the front doorbell rang.

"That must be the girls," Andrea adjusted one last glass.

Andrea and Bailey went to the front entry to let in the wedding planning committee. Viviane, Carrie, Grace, Tiffany, and Laura walked through the door chattering away, barely pausing for hugs and hellos.

"Chinese food's in the kitchen and then we can set up in the dining room to plan the rest of this wedding." Andrea hugged each of the girls.

While everyone grabbed a plate and moved to the dining room, Bailey told Andrea about her wedding dress problem standing in the food line. "Grace and I have been through her entire shop, and there's nothing that could be ready in the short amount of time I have that will work."

Grace sighed mid-bite of a dumpling, while she waited to get a drink. "I own a wedding dress shop and of course, my best friend can't find a single dress in it that will work." Smirking at her best friend, Grace fussed, "I feel like a failure."

"Sorry, Gracie, but I have a specific dress in mind. Now, I'm just not sure it will happen, since I need it before December."

"What are you wanting exactly?" Andrea inquired sitting down with her plate of food.

"I wanted something short, white, like this..." Bailey reached into her purse and pulled out a picture of a simple 50s style wedding dress with an A-line skirt ending just above the knees. "It's what I've always wanted. The dress I got for the wedding to Preston was longer with lots and lots of lace." Bailey rolled her eyes. "His mother insisted I wear something more formal and fitting for my new station in life."

"You should always get the dress you want, not what the mother or bridesmaids want you to get," Grace slapped her hand on the island. *I hate it when poor brides get run over by family and friend's wishes.*

"Umm, Bailey?"

"Yes, Andrea?"

"That looks just like my wedding dress." Holding the picture closely, Andrea noticed the small details and simple lines. *That's the dress I wore to marry my handsome James thirty years ago. I can't believe my future daughter would want my dream dress.*

"You're kidding!" Bailey raised an eyebrow.

Snorting, Andrea got up and walked out of the room. She returned a moment later carrying a photo album. Opening to one of the first pages, she handed the book to Bailey. "That's me in my dress. Even though it was the eighties, I'd always loved the dress from Audrey Hepburn's *Funny Face*. I had my mother sew something similar for my wedding. She was grateful in the end because it was much easier to make in comparison to what was the style at the time."

Bailey looked at the photo and couldn't believe her eyes. She found herself staring at a younger Andrea in the exact dress from her clipping, smiling adoringly at a young man who looked a lot like Josh. Very dashing in his uniform, James looked down at Andrea with love in his dark green eyes. "It IS the same dress. A few details are different but you're right, it's the dress!"

"It's too bad you still don't have it, Andrea, because you two are similar in size and it would be easy to fit it for Bales." Viviane glanced at the picture. Looking back up at the group, "You really could be mother and daughter."

"I do have it." Andrea turned to Bailey, "I don't know how you'd feel wearing my dress, but you're more than welcome to have it for your big day." Whispering, she continued, "If you want to that is..."

Bailey felt tears welling up in her eyes. "Of course, I would want to wear it. I can't believe you'd let me... I..."

Hugging the young woman to stop her protest, Andrea insisted, "I'd be honored to have my daughter wear my dress."

The entire group of ladies all teared up as Andrea ran upstairs to the guest bedroom closet to grab the box her gown had been packed in. Carrying the box downstairs, she thought as she passed James photo, *you'd be proud of our son. He picked a wonderful young woman.*

While Bailey went to another room to try on the wedding gown, Andrea and the other women wrote out a list of everything that needed to be done before the big day. Struggling to focus, Andrea remembered her own wedding. It was in June and she had felt like the luckiest bride to be marrying tall, handsome Gunnery Sergeant James Timothy Cabot. *I don't remember too many details, like who all was there and what everyone wore, I mostly remember being so proud to walk down the aisle to my James. I enjoyed every moment of that special day, and want the same for Bailey and Josh.*

Dividing up the list, no one noticed at first when Bailey stepped back into the room until Carrie exclaimed, "Oh, Bales, it looks great on you."

Andrea turned and saw the smile on Bailey's face and knew the young woman had found her dream dress. Walking up to hug her, Andrea agreed, "It's perfect." *Lord, let her look back on her wedding day with the same happiness I do thinking about my special day marrying James.*

Bailey could only nod, trying to keep the tears from falling on her dress. Grace walked around, tucking and rearranging. "It really doesn't need anything, but a tuck here and there. It's in great condition, Andrea."

"Well, now the dress part is done, we need to get the rest of the wedding planned," Bailey let out a huge sigh of relief. "This was the only thing I was worried about after all of Grace's stories over the years of brides who waited until the last minute."

"I do have some crazy stories." Grace smirked. "But, I'll save them for another girl's night out. I don't want to scare our bride-to-be."

"Thanks, Gracie."

Carrie smiled at the group. "Well, it's a good thing God already had the dress part planned out so you don't have to stress Bales."

Bailey laughed, "God's good, because it turns out, Andrea's mom made the perfect dress for me thirty years ago!"

While everyone laughed, Bailey ran to change and put the gown lovingly back in its box. "Soon," she ran her hands down the satin fabric, "I'll be wearing you very soon."

As she started walking back to the dining room, she could hear gales of laughter. *I'm glad God gave me such wonderful friends to be part of my family. I'm still praying for my parents and I'm trusting God about them. The invitations should be ready this time next week. It's only a small wedding with under thirty people. I'll mail my parents an invitation with a note saying how much I hope they'll come. God must have a reason for my calls not going through.*

Turning the corner, Bailey paused in the hall listening to the laughter, before joining in to plan for her special day. *December seventh can't come fast enough for me, either! I just pray my parents come for the special day.*

"Okay ladies, let's plan this wedding." Bailey sat at the dinning table feeling peace about her parents.

Mark's Journal Entry – October 19, 2013

Lord,

I think I found a way to get the birthday invitation to Noah's little friend, Andrea. Please help me find favor with the right people. Noah will be devasted if he never sees her again.

Chapter Five

"This has been a great planning session. We're organized for the rest of this year all the way into February of the next," Andrea raised her glass of tea. "And all done the week before Thanksgiving to boot."

Bailey clinked her glass against Andrea's before replying, "I was worried Josh and I would need to delay our honeymoon, because of the Christmas dinner we're catering a few days after the wedding, but since we've planned out the meal and I'll have recipes for you and Noelle…"

"Don't worry, Bales. It will be fine. It's a small Sunday school class from church and we'll follow your recipes exactly. Piece of cake."

"It's funny how I'm only truly organized when it comes to cooking," Bailey smirked.

Andrea closed her notebook. "It's good for my son to have more… let's say upheaval in his life."

Bailey laughed holding her side. "I've tried warning him about my lack of housekeeping abilities, but he swears as long as I keep him in his favorite muffins, he'll deal with the chaos."

As the two women laughed, Bailey heard her phone ringing and reached into her purse. Sure it was Josh, she put in on speaker for Andrea. "Hello, Josh."

"Bailey? It's Preston, not Josh."

"Hi, Preston. It's good to hear from you. Did you get the sermons Josh sent you? He said they'd probably be delivered today or tomorrow. He's been working on the sound committee at church and thought you'd like some of the special Wednesday services not on the website."

"No, but I'll keep a look out for the package to arrive. I was actually calling because I hear congratulations are in order."

Bailey wrinkled her forehead. "Did you talk to Josh?"

"No, your parents called me to ask if I knew you were getting married to some Josh fellow."

Bailey reached for Andrea's hand. "Oh really? They never called me about the invitation I sent. I was starting to wonder if they had gotten it."

Preston didn't speak a moment and Bailey started to wonder if they had been cut off. "Preston? Are you still there? Hello?"

Clearing his throat, Preston said, "Umm, Bales... I don't know how to tell you this, but from what they said to me today... They aren't planning on attending the wedding."

Tears started to fall down Bailey's cheeks, and Andrea moved around the table to put her arm around her after texting Josh to come to the kitchen quickly. *He's only in the carriage house, but I hope he gets here soon.*

Tears clogged her throat and Bailey was barely able to choke out, "They're not... not planning on coming to my wedding?!?"

"I'm sorry, Bales. It seems they're angry about you getting married so quickly after our breakup. I only know about it, because they called me asking about who was this Josh fellow."

"Oh..." Bailey didn't speak but felt more tears slide down her cheeks as Josh came through the back door.

Seeing Bailey was upset, he came and put his arms around her, while Preston continued to speak. "... I told them Josh was a great guy and I was happy for both of you, but they refused to listen. They actually hung up on me."

Hiccupping, Bailey said, "I guess... I guess I should be happy then..."

Everyone gasped and Josh asked, "Happy, B? Really?"

"Yeah, because they've never gotten upset about something I've done before. Even when I refused to go to law school, they just cut me off and stopped talking to me. At least this time they reacted with some type of feeling."

"Bales, I want you to know I've never said anything negative about you or Josh to your parents. I'm very happy for both of you and know you two are meant to be together." Preston paused, but then gushed over the phone, "God's been opening my eyes about a lot of things, and I've actually been praying for a godly woman of my own. I just know I want to be a stronger Christian before I get into that type of relationship."

Josh spoke up, "Preston, we know you wouldn't say anything negative. We actually mailed you an invitation to the wedding and it will be arriving with some Wednesday night sermons I've taped for you. Bailey and I talked and we'd like to you to come to the wedding if you can make the trip down here from Colorado Springs."

"Really?" Preston was quiet for a moment, "Thank you, I'd be honored."

Smiling through her tears, Bailey nodded, "Besides Grace, you're the closest I'll have to family in attendance. Josh and I would be honored if you would come and stand in for my family."

"I'll be there. December seventh, isn't it?"

"Seventeen days!" Josh said, before kissing Bailey. "I've been counting down since the day after I proposed."

Bailey giggled, "He's not kidding, either. I said I wanted a short engagement and he asked does December work?"

Andrea piped in, "They're trying to overwhelm me with planning a wedding in under two months, but everyone's been a big help."

"Well, let me know if I can do anything. I'll fly in a few days early and help you set up or anything else you might need. I'm honored to be considered part of Bailey's family and will do whatever I can to help out."

"Thank you, Preston." Josh squeezed Bailey's hand. "We'll see you soon."

After a round of goodbyes, Bailey ended the call and sat for a moment, still reeling from the fact her parents weren't coming to her wedding. Leaning against Josh, Bailey cried, praying this was a part of God's plan to save her parents.

Neither Josh nor Bailey noticed Andrea leave the room. It wasn't until a few minutes later Andrea walked over holding a small gift bag. "Bailey?"

Lifting her head, Bailey said through her tears, "Yes?"

"I have something I want to give you. I was going to wait until your wedding day, but I think now would be better after that phone call."

When Bailey reached for the gift, Andrea said, "In my family for five generations, the oldest daughter was bestowed a special ring on her wedding day. I received it from my mother, who was given it by her mother, and so on. It's been a tradition for many years and has never been broken."

Bailey looked at Andrea with a puzzled look on her face but didn't speak as she said, "After I had Jacob, there were complications and I wasn't able to have any more children. I was heartbroken because I knew the ring tradition would end with me."

Moving to sit by Bailey at the kitchen table, Andrea nodded for her to open the gift. "I realized a few weeks ago God had given me a daughter, a best friend, and business partner all in one. I took the ring I've been wearing since the day I was married to a jeweler and had them put the stone into a pendant necklace for you."

Bailey opened the bag to find a small necklace box of blue velvet, with fresh tears in her eyes, she opened the box to find a beautiful emerald in an elegant filigree setting on a simple silver chain.

"I know you can't wear rings when you're cooking, but I wanted you to be able to wear this constantly and KNOW you're truly the daughter I prayed for and never thought I'd have."

"Andrea..." Tears falling in rivers down her cheeks, Bailey croaked, "I don't know what to say."

"I never thought of giving the ring to my daughter-in-law, but I knew I could give it to you, the daughter of my heart. I did not give birth to you, but I love you like family and not just because you're marrying my son. This necklace is to be a reminder you're not only a part of my family but a part of my heart."

Bailey fell into Andrea's arms, sobbing her thanks. Andrea patted her back, comforting the young woman, thankful she was in her life.

After a moment, Bailey sat back and said, "Would you help me put it on?"

"Of course, dear."

After Andrea clasped it around her neck, Bailey reached her hand out to touch the necklace and then looked at Andrea, a sweet smile on her tear stained cheeks. "Thank you, Mom. I'll treasure it always, at least until I give it to my daughter, your granddaughter one day."

"That would make me very happy," Andrea felt tears of her own falling.

The rest of the day, whenever Bailey felt sad about her parents, she held onto the necklace and thanked God for bringing her to Cartersville.

Mark Hastings stared at the invitation his grandson had made out to Andrea with his favorite blue crayon. He smiled to think even a few months later, Noah hadn't given up on having her come to his birthday party on December fourteenth. The boy had been asking every few days if anyone had come up with a plan to get Andrea to his party. Becka, Noah's mom was unsure how to get the invitation to someone who they didn't even have a last name for, let alone the child's parents' names.

When his grandson begged him to find a way to invite his friend, Mark eventually came up with a plan to take the invitation to the physical therapist's office and have them mail it. It would keep Andrea's information private, but still, give her parents the option to bring the little girl to the party.

Pleased with his plan, he pulled into the physical therapy parking lot and made his way into the lobby. Praying the receptionist would help him with his plan to cheer up his grandson, he took a deep breath.

"Hi, I'm Mark Hastings. Noah's grandfather." He smiled at the woman behind the counter, hoping to charm her. "I'm hoping you could help me. I have a birthday invitation for Andrea. I'm not sure what her last name is or her parents, but my grandson Noah wants to invite her to his birthday party in December. They met here this summer and became fast friends."

The young brunette looked at him perplexed and stated loudly, "Look MISTER, I don't know any Andrea. I'm a temp subbing for the usual lady who works here because she's out on maternity leave." The woman's voice turned shrill, "I do KNOW we can't give out a patient's information, especially a child's address!"

Raising his hands in hopes of calming down the irate woman, Mark quickly explained, "I figured that, but thought you could mail it to the address you have down for her and then if she was able to come, she could." *Keep it simple, Mark. You don't want to get arrested.*

The receptionist still seemed upset, and Mark found himself praying for divine help. *I can't let Noah down. He's been a bit depressed since he hasn't been able to see his friend in months.*

Just as he was about to give up, a young woman he recognized as Noah's therapist walked up to the front, and Mark smiled with relief. *Please Lord, let this woman help me.*

"I'm ready for the next patient." Looking up at him, Kristy waved. "Oh, hello, Mr. Hastings. Is everything okay with Noah?"

"Yes, he's fine, but missing his friend, Andrea."

"Oh, yes. I'm sure he is. I've never seen two people get along as fast and as well as those two did."

Pleased this woman seemed to understand, Mark explained the dilemma he was in with the invitation and no address.

"Sure," Kristy nodded, "That shouldn't be a problem. It won't be breaking any rules if we mail the invite for you. Andrea's information stays protected, and Noah gets the chance to invite her to his birthday party."

"Exactly." Sighing with relief, Mark gushed, "Thank you! Noah's been despondent since he hasn't seen her in so long."

"Don't worry about it. Tell Noah I said hi and I hope he's keeping up his exercises. I know he'll be wanting to play soccer soon."

"He's itching to start." Handing the invitation to the young woman, Mark said his goodbyes.

Walking back to his jeep, he mused, *I believe Kip Saturn would be impressed with the way we've gone about hunting down the hero's girl.*

Thinking about his new series based on his grandson, Mark thought of something he should add to the scene he was working on and was itching to get back to his computer before he had to pick his grandson up from school. *Robot NOAH and the real Noah will be pleased with my efforts for the day, part of a rough draft done and I found a way to save the girl, so to speak.*

Chapter Six

"Nervous?"

Bailey looked up at Andrea and unclenched her hands. "A little." She turned to face her soon to be official mother. "It's not like last time, I know I'm marrying the right man, a godly man...."

"But you wish your parents were here?"

"Yes, and it's silly because I should stop expecting them to be the parents I want and accept them as they are."

"It's not wrong to want more of a relationship with them. You just can't put your life on hold waiting for them to change." Andrea touched the side of Bailey's face, before dropping her hand to adjust the emerald pendant. "We'll keep praying for them and take lots of pictures for them to see when they're ready."

"Thank you, Andrea."

Hands on her hips, Andrea explained, "You should be running upstairs to put on your wedding gown. The ceremony will be starting before you know it and the photographer wants to get some photos of you and Grace." Chuckling, Andrea continued, "Since it's such a small ceremony with only Grace as your maid of honor, and Aiden as Josh's best man, pictures will be a breeze."

Bailey smiled, "It's been easy to plan because we had to make decisions fast."

Seeing a photo of Jacob and Josh arm in arm, she thought of her youngest whom she hadn't spoken to in months. Andrea sighed, "I wish we could have gotten in contact with Jacob, but he's on some long-term mission and is unreachable right now." Andrea smiled, a wistful look in her eyes, "But it's okay. Aiden's stepping in for Jacob and I trust God's keeping my boy safe."

"I'm praying for my brother-in-law's safety as well." Hugging the worried Mom, Bailey continued, "Don't worry. And I'll be right up. I just want to get something to drink before I put on a white dress."

"Do you want me to get you something?"

"No, I'll be up in a minute. I'll see you there. I want you and Grace to help me get ready. You're my family and the bride's family is supposed to help her get dressed."

"See you in a minute, then."

"Thanks, Mom."

"I'll never get tired of hearing that." Andrea winked before marching upstairs to the redone master suite Bailey and Josh would share once they were back from their honeymoon.

"I'll never get tired of saying it," Bailey stepped into the kitchen, walking to the fridge, turning and nearly stumbled into someone. "Josh, what are you doing here?"

"I wanted to see you." Josh could see the worry in her eyes, which had been lurking for a few days now. "How are you?"

"Everyone keeps asking me that." Looking at Josh, she felt peace wash over her as she stepped into his outstretched arms. "I'm telling myself to be brave, but I don't know how I feel about walking down the aisle by myself."

"I thought as much. When we had the rehearsal dinner last night, I could see it hurt you not to have your parents here."

Only nodding, because she refused to cry sad tears on her wedding day, Bailey stared out the window to the barn recently decorated for their wedding and it reminded her of Josh's efforts to have it decorated for their make-up dinner and proposal.

"I have an idea, B."

At the sound of his special nickname for her, Bailey turned back to stare into his vivid green eyes. *I do love this man, Lord. He's most definitely the one.*

"At the rehearsal dinner, we had several people stand and give speeches, and I was touched by Preston's speech. When he said coming to win you back brought him to the Lord and made him a brother in Christ to a wonderful group of people, I couldn't have been happier."

Leaning against Josh, Bailey sighed. "Yes, it's crazy how much he's changed. I realized it when he got here a few days early and has been such a big help."

Bailey felt Josh laugh as he held her. "I know, it's crazy to think I invited your ex-fiancé to my bachelor party, but he's becoming a good friend."

"God does have a funny sense of humor."

"I'm glad you think so... what if Preston walked you down the aisle?"

Bailey leaned back, unsure if her current fiancé was joking. "Preston?" *I do think of him as more of a brother than an ex. He's become a great friend over the past few months and he has really been growing in the Lord.*

"I mentioned it to him, and he said he'd be honored, but only if you're okay with the idea."

Hugging Josh, Bailey sighed with contentment. "Thank you. I think that would be perfect."

"I'll go tell him. He'll meet you at the foot of the stairs to walk you over."

"Thanks, Josh. You're a thoughtful, kind man."

Kissing her, Josh smiled. "You're the reason why. I'll see you soon and then you'll be Mrs. Josh Cabot."

"I can't wait."

"Bailey are you ready?"

Bailey looked down the stairs and saw Preston in his dark gray suit and smiled, *the irony isn't lost on me, Lord.* Nodding, she said, "Yes."

Carefully walking down the stairway, Bailey reached the bottom and took Preston's outstretched arm. "Thank you for walking me down the aisle and standing in for my parents."

Looking into Bailey's shining green eyes, Preston paused in their walk. "Bailey, I'm the one who's honored. I'm a completely different man from the one you were engaged too, and I'm better for having known you. I'm sorry your parents aren't here, but I'm honored you're allowing me to walk you down the aisle."

Touched by his words, Bailey blinked back tears. "God works in mysterious ways, but I know there's someone special out there for you. I've been praying you find her and have your happily ever after, too!"

"Thank you, Bales, but first, we need to get you married."

Laughing, Bailey let him escort her to the barn entrance. Seeing the lights shining on several rows of friends and family waiting for her, she felt content. Looking for Josh, she smiled to see he was cleaning his glasses while waiting for her to come into view.

Walking down the aisle, she only had eyes for him. After Preston placed her hands in Josh's outstretched ones, Bailey winked at Preston before turning to her future husband. Pastor Graham started the ceremony, but it seemed to fly by while staring into Josh's eyes. Soon the pastor asked them to say their vows and nodded for Josh to start.

Josh cleared his throat, and slowly started speaking, "Bailey Dawn Evans when we met, you dropped hot cheesy pasta all over me and ruined an expensive suit and shoes."

Quiet laughter broke out in the crowd, many knowing the funny story. Josh continued, "I should've known then I was in for it, but I stubbornly refused to see you for who you really are. You're funny, smart, the most amazing cook, sweet, but feisty. You hate spiders of all kinds, slow drivers, and people who don't take proper care of their ovens."

The crowd was really laughing now and Josh smiled. "You hate to clean unless it's your kitchen and you love using your talents for the Lord. You embraced my mother as your own and taught me what selfless love truly is and while I can never explain my love for you, I promise to spend the rest of my life trying. I promise to love you when you're sick, tired, or hungry. I promise to love you when the oven breaks and you still have to get a meal out for three hundred people. I promise to be a kinder, more loving man because you remind me of God's grace and blessings every day you smile at me. I promise to be by your side until my last breath on this earth. I love you."

The crowd was in tears at Josh's words, and Bailey felt a river sliding down her own cheeks. *Wow. How am I to follow that?!?*

Pastor Graham nodded to Bailey and she took a deep breath, "Josh, when we met, I was expecting a teenage boy and what I got was an angry man who wasn't thrilled I was here…"

Pausing, Bailey remembered where they started and how far they had come, truly humbled by God's handiwork. "Now, that I have gotten to know you and your heart, I better understand your protectiveness and loyalty. I am truly blessed to call you mine and I promise to love your quirks, from muttering while you work on the computer, cleaning your glasses when you're nervous, to the incessant need to buy lots of computer equipment. I promise to remind you when things get tough, God has a plan. When we fight, I promise to not to let your stubbornness keep us from following the path God has for us."

Andrea snorted, but Bailey kept speaking with a wink at Josh. "I promise to cherish your kind heart and generosity to others."

Wiping a tear, Bailey took a calming breath, "I promise to love you every day and to stand by you in the good and bad times, knowing the bad times will not always last. I promise to trust in your love for me and I promise to be by your side until my last breath on this earth. I love you."

The crowd had quieted down with Bailey's words and even Pastor Graham had to pause after the couple's sweet vows. After a moment, he had them exchange rings and with a prayer of blessings, he said to the crowd, "I present to you, Mr. and Mrs. Joshua Cabot."

With cheers and shouts, the crowd stood to their feet clapping for the married couple. Bailey looked around and smiled to see everyone happy for her. Winking at Andrea, she and Josh walked down the aisle ready to celebrate long into the night.

"Can I have this dance, Mom?"

Andrea turned to her son and felt tears rise up seeing him in his tuxedo. *We did good, James.*

She smiled while stepping into his open arms. "I haven't seen you alone too much tonight. You're either holding on to Bailey or Jax."

Josh laughed, "I've got to hold the little guy while I can. Every time I see him, he's gotten so much bigger. Not even four months old and I think my godson's going to be a linebacker."

"Growing is what babies do."

"We'll be leaving soon and I wanted to have a few minutes to tell you I love you and I'm so thankful you brought Bailey to Cartersville. Thank you for NOT listening to me."

Andrea stopped dancing and stood still, unable to hold back the tears in her brown eyes. "Oh, Josh, I couldn't be more pleased or surprised with how everything worked out. God is so good."

"Yes, He is," Josh looked over at his new bride, talking with Viviane and Delia Anne. *It's amazing what happens when you let God work His plan and not the one you had in mind.*

After the dance ended, Josh kissed his mother on the cheek, before moving to grab Bailey for one last dance before they left for Massachusetts. It was a surprise for her because she had always wanted to go there, and Josh knew she missed snow. *God is good because I checked the weather earlier and it will be snowing when we arrive.*

As Andrea watched her son twirl his new bride around the dance floor, she sighed. *Lord, it's so good to see how this worked out, and in a way no one expected.*

The entire day reminded her of her own wedding. Seeing Bailey walk down the aisle in the same dress she wore to meet James, made her think of the widow's meeting talk about dating and marriage. She was happy for the young couple, but at this point in her life, now that James was gone, she wasn't sure if she'd consider dating and re-marrying. *I mean, Lord, I loved James Cabot but he could be a bit strict and demanding. I need to be honest about our relationship, and while we had a good marriage, I can see now in hindsight he could be a bit overbearing and overprotective. I love my life now, especially since You brought Bailey into our lives. I just can't imagine having another man in my life who I'd have to run everything I do by.*

Grace came running up to Andrea, her green bridesmaid dress billowing behind her. "They're getting ready to go. I've got bubbles for you. I thought you'd want to be near the end of the line to send them off."

"I couldn't imagine being anywhere else."

Andrea, feeling content, went outside to stand by the limo taking the young couple to the airport. Waving bubbles a few moments later, Andrea felt happy tears on her cheeks and thought, *Lord, I have a wonderful life.*

Chapter Seven

"Oh, Muffin what a week! Thank goodness Bailey and Josh are back tomorrow." Petting the dog who had jumped up beside her on the couch, Andrea stared out the large front window of what she fondly called her little cottage.

"Sleeping in this morning was wonderful. With Bailey gone on her honeymoon, I had an excellent reminder this week of why I brought her on in the first place."

She smiled down at her little dog, who licked Andrea's arm and wagged her tail in response. Andrea continued to pat Muffin's head while she continued speaking out loud, "We'll have a quiet Saturday, then church in the morning and before we know it, the house will be full of people again."

Andrea picked up a large stack of mail she had been ignoring, because of the wedding and covering the catering jobs with Noelle for the past week. She kept meaning to look through and sort, but each night after she had gotten home, she only had enough energy to fix dinner for herself and feed Muffin. Rifling through the pile, she sorted bills and business from Bailey and Josh's mail. *I can't believe she'll be living here starting tomorrow. I'm a blessed woman!*

Seeing a large envelope from her physical therapist's office, she frowned. "I shouldn't have any outstanding bills, Muffin. I haven't been since September and it's already December fourteenth."

Opening the envelope, she was puzzled to find a smaller card inside with her name written in blue crayon. Reading the invitation, she smiled.

You are invited to an
OUT OF THIS WORLD 8th BIRTHDAY PARTY
for
Noah Hastings
When: December 14th
Where: Noah's House
Time: 3-5 pm
Please RSVP

Andrea looked at her watch. "It's already after eleven, girl. I've got to hurry if I'm going to make it and buy a gift."

Not rising from the couch, Muffin watched her sprint to the bedroom to change. The dog didn't raise her head but settled in for a nap while Andrea frantically thought of a special gift for her friend. "I want to get him something perfect, Muffin. I know he loves to read, especially science fiction stories." Throwing on a long-sleeved top in a pretty mauve color that set off the highlights the salon added to her hair, she wondered if she had ever heard Noah mention the Kip series Mark Lawson wrote. *I read it over and over to both my boys growing up. They loved Kip stories! I wonder if I could find the complete set to give as a gift? I know Noah would love them, too!*

Putting on some dark jeans and hopping on one foot as she put on ballet slippers, Andrea ran through her living room to grab her purse and cut through the main house to the garage. *Lord, help me find those novels. There are about twenty books in the series now, and I'd love to get him the complete set.*

Andrea threw her car in reverse and rushed out to the interstate, determined to scourer the countryside until she found all of the books. *I've got until two to find them and get home to wrap up the gift since I don't want to be late to the birthday party I'm planning on crashing.*

Andrea pulled up to the curve of the subdivision listed on the invite. She wasn't surprised by all of the cars, she knew Noah had lots of friends. *He's such an engaging boy and reminds me so much of my two when they were younger.*

Reaching to grab the large box she had wrapped his gift in, Andrea hesitated to get out of the car. *I can't believe I'm showing up at this party without accepting the invitation and on top of it I'm late. My grandmother would be appalled.* As she walked up the front steps, she could hear children playing outside, even in the cooler weather.

After knocking on the door, Andrea prayed Noah's mother wouldn't be upset she was crashing the birthday party. Before she finished her prayer, the bright blue door opened with a yank as a pretty golden-brown haired woman yelled, "I've got it." Turning to Andrea, she raised an eyebrow, not recognizing the parent of one of her son's school friends, "Hello! Are you here for Noah's birthday party?"

Andrea smiled while holding up the large box covered in planets and stars. "Yes, I'm Andrea Cabot."

"You're Andrea?!?" The woman's mouth fell open and it took her a few seconds before she asked sharply, "THE Andrea from physical therapy?"

"Yes, that's me." Brows raised, Andrea shifted on her feet. "Didn't Noah invite me?"

Realizing she was being rude and making the poor woman uncomfortable, Noah's mom quickly ushered Andrea through the door. "I'm so sorry. The way Noah's talked about you all these months... well, we all thought you were the same age."

"Ohh." Andrea's cheeks turned red and her hands flew to her mouth. "I'm flattered he thinks so highly of me. Noah does remind me greatly of my boys when they were little. Now they're almost 30..."

"Wait... your sons are in their late 20s...?" Looking the woman up and down, Noah's mother marveled. *She looks like maybe early 40s and I honestly thought at first glance she was in her late 30s with the brown bob and highlights. Lord, can I look this good when I'm her age?!?*

Blush spreading, Andrea said, "I get told a lot I don't look my age, and it has led to problems before, but I can't say I've ever been mistaken for a small child, though."

Noah's mom looked into Andrea's brown eyes and could see the kindness reflected there. *She must have a soft spot for Noah since she bought him such a big gift. He struggles to have any close friends, he's not shy, but can't seem to really connect with kids his own age since we moved to Georgia. We were hoping... well, that's no reason to make this poor woman feel uncomfortable.*

"Please forgive my manners, Andrea. I'm Becka Hastings, Noah's mom." Extending her hand, she shook Andrea's before pointing her to the living room. "Everyone's outside running off some energy before cake and presents. I'm sure you heard all the noise coming up the driveway."

Andrea laughed softly, "It's the sign of a good party."

"Yes, I wasn't planning on them running outside since it had been raining earlier, but that many kids can only stay in the playroom for so long."

Walking through the back door, Andrea saw around fifteen boys and girls playing tag. Standing around on the porch, a handful of adults watched while bundled in coats to ward off the chill.

"Please meet my husband." Becka took Andrea's gift and put it on a long table overflowing with presents. Andrea turned to a tall man with dark blond hair as Becka called over her shoulder, "Honey, this is Andrea, Noah's friend from PT."

Mr. Hastings turned to Andrea and was unable to speak as his jaw dropped. "Um... Andrea?" He strangled out, holding out his hand.

Good grief, what's Noah been telling these people?!?

"Hi, I'm Ki..." Noah's dad paused, "You look very familiar..." He started at her a few moments, and then his face lighting up, he cried out, "Mrs. Cabot, right? Hip surgery in June?"

"Yes!" Andrea nodded.

"I was the doctor who did your surgery."

"Oh, yes. I seem to remember your face, but I'm afraid I was a little out of it at the time."

"It's understandable." He chuckled, "Well that explains why you were in PT with Noah."

"Mrs. Andrea! You came!"

A loud shout interrupted the conversation and before Andrea could completely turn around, she was enveloped in a tight hug. "I knew Grandpa would find you."

"Happy Birthday, Mr. Noah. I'm glad you found a way to invite me. Your Grandpa's pretty smart to get me the invitation the way he did."

"He's a genius, all right!"

"Where is he? I'd like to finally meet him."

"He had to get more ice. Dad forgot." Leaning forward to whisper in Andrea's ear, Noah giggled. "Dad forgets things a lot. Mom says it's 'cause he's too smart for his own good."

Hugging Noah, Andrea smiled, "Well, when your Grandpa gets here, make sure you introduce me." *I'm interested to finally meet the man Noah considers such a hero.*

"Deal."

Noah hoped Grandpa showed up soon. *I've been waiting for months to have Grandpa meet Mrs. Andrea.*

Becka walked over to Noah and put her arm around his small shoulders. "Sweetie, we should open gifts now. You've got a pile and by then Grandpa should have ice for us to have drinks with the cake and ice cream."

"Okay, Mom." Running to call his classmates inside, he paused at the screen door to turn to Andrea, "You can sit by me while I open gifts."

Becka turned to Andrea who nodded yes to Noah's statement. "Can I get you something to drink?"

"Water's fine."

Pointing to the table, Becka waved for her to sit down. "Noah will open gifts at the table."

"Thank you."

Moving to sit, Andrea tried to remember Noah's dad's name. *It was something with a K. I seem to remember how much I liked the name.*

Before it came to mind, Andrea's thoughts were interrupted by the excited group of kids running in. After everyone settled down, Noah started opening his presents, and as Andrea sipped on her water, she kept running through names starting with a K in her head.

She didn't stop until Noah pulled her gift in front of him and started to unwrap it. Andrea watched carefully until she heard someone with a deep voice say, "Kip, here are your keys."

"Thanks, Dad. Noah's been asking when you'd be back."

Andrea turned to see the Grandpa, Noah had been gushing about for months and was horrified when she recognized him. *Dear Lord, Noah's grandfather is Mark Lawson! He's the famous author who wrote the Kip series I read to my sons!*

Thinking of her surgery, she remembered she thought it was strange her doctor was named after a book character. *I just thought it was the pain pills and I misunderstood.* Realizing he was the same man, she cringed. *The awful fact is, my orthopedic doctor was the inspiration for the young Kip series. I remember Mark Lawson said he named the character after his own son in an interview I read years ago.*

Turning back quickly to Noah about to open her gift, she cringed, *Noah probably owns every Kip book ever written directly from the author himself. Oh NO!! I don't think I could have brought a worse gift if I tried.*

Noah opened his present and started giggling. Andrea looked at him and grinned as they both broke out in gales of laughter. Everyone stopped to stare, but the two were laughing so hard, tears running down their faces, they were unable to explain. After a moment, Noah asked Andrea, "You didn't know? I can't believe I never..."

"No, silly boy. You always talked about the Neurological Optimal Animatronic Humanoid- NOAH being written about you, not your famous grandfather who already had two hit series based on your dad."

Blushing, Noah shrugged, "I guess I forgot."

Ruffling his hair, Andrea smirked, "Yeah, well..."

Kip asked Noah, "Son, what's going on?"

Turning to his dad, Noah pointed, "Mrs. Andrea bought me the entire Kip series because she knew I loved sci-fi."

"... and since he never mentioned the Kip series, I thought he'd enjoy them!"

Later when Noah continued to open gifts and talk with his classmates, Mark Lawson walked over to Andrea and held out his hand. "Hi, I'm Mark Lawson Hastings. My middle name is my mother's maiden name, which I used as my pen name to keep my writing and family life separate."

"I'm learning that." Smiling into his bright aqua eyes, Andrea shook his hand. "It's very nice to meet you. I've been a fan of yours for many years. I read my boys the Kip series for young adults and loved them so much, I started secretly reading the adult Kip series."

Mark tried to hide his laughter, "You're a bit older than we were led to believe."

"I'm learning that, too. Apparently, no one knew I had two sons almost in their thirties and wasn't another elementary school kid."

"Sons in their thirties?!?"

Sighing, Andrea winked at Becka, who was listening closely to the conversation. "I keep getting that, too."

Holding out her hand, Andrea said, "Hello, my name is Andrea Cora Cabot. I run a catering business with my daughter and have two sons who are almost thirty, and I'm turning fifty-one in about two weeks."

Mark stood there unable to speak a moment, before shaking his head. "It's very nice to meet you. My grandson thinks very highly of you."

Looking over at Noah opening up his last gift, Andrea sighed, "I'm pretty fond of him myself. He's a sweet kid and made PT bearable with his cheerful spirit."

Mark looked at the beautiful woman before him and could see why Noah was taken with her. *She's beautiful and sweet. No wonder my grandson has a little crush on this lady.* Looking at her out of the corner of his eye, he thought, *if things were different, I might have a crush on her, too!*

As Andrea helped Becka hand out cake, Mark watched Andrea's graceful movements. *Who would have thought we'd only be three years apart in age?!? Boy, does my grandson know how to pick them!*

Mark's Journal Entry - December 14, 2013

Lord,

I met Noah's crush, Andrea today. She's nothing like we thought. It turns out she's closer to my age than Noah's. I don't know who was more shocked - me or Becka. Poor Andrea! It must have been hard for her seeing the surprise on everyone's faces all afternoon.

After the party, Noah asked what I thought of his friend and I didn't miss Kip choking on his drink or Becka's raised eyebrows. This isn't the first time I've been asked what I thought of a woman, but it is the first time I've been asked by my eight-year-old grandson! I can't tell if he's playing matchmaker or not, but now Becka has a twinkle in her eye every time Andrea's name is mentioned.

Now, Lord, I promised when I started writing in these journals in the 90s, I would always be honest. And if things were different, if I were different, there would be a twinkle my eyes and I would have asked Andrea on a date before Noah blew the candles out on his birthday cake...

But we both know that's not possible for me to do. I had my chance at a wife and I blew it. We both know how and why. As much as I might like to date Andrea, I know it isn't going to happen. Please help me to forget her. I can't sleep, I keep seeing her smiling face, so I got up and tried to write, but couldn't concentrate... I keep hearing her musical laughter run through my head.

Chapter Eight

"Have fun this morning, Mom. We'll see you this evening for dinner." Bailey hugged Andrea before following Josh out the door. "I'm sorry we didn't know the toy drive was this morning when we signed up to help..."

"Don't worry, Bales. I'll see you both later. You don't have to spend every moment of my birthday with me. I've got a few things I want to do before the party tonight."

"What party?" Bailey abruptly stopped walking, trying to look puzzled.

"Oh, you!" Hands waving, Andrea snorted, "I heard both of you talking about who to invite days ago."

"Well, a birthday's a big deal and you know I love an excuse to cook."

"I'm not used to big celebrations for my birthday. I'm a December baby, as close to Christmas as you can get with it being on the twenty-third. Most people are out of town...."

Running back through the door, Bailey hugged Andrea tight. "Don't worry, Mom. I've planned a simple evening with good friends and good food. Everyone wants the chance to celebrate you and everything you do for us."

Hearing a honking horn, Bailey sighed, "It's a good thing I'm already married to the man. I knew he was a stickler for being on time, but good grief! He has to know I don't know the meaning of on time unless I'm catering an event."

Andrea laughed as Bailey went out the door fussing at Josh. *They're so cute together.*

Reaching down to pat Muffin on the head, Andrea said, "Well Muffin, how would you like to celebrate my birthday this morning?"

Muffin wagged her tail, but Andrea looked at her hands clapped them together. "A manicure and pedicure would be nice. Then maybe a long walk after I get back?"

Before she could make a decision, she heard her phone ringing and rushed to grab it off the kitchen counter. "Hello," Andrea out of breath, didn't look to see who was calling.

"Mrs. Andrea? It's Noah."

"Hi, Noah. How are you?"

"Good. I wanted to see if you and Muffin wanted to go with me and Grandpa to walk at Dellinger Park. Since I'm out of school for Christmas break, Grandpa says I need to run off some energy and I really want to meet your new dog."

Andrea laughed, remembering her own boys struggling with pent-up energy during the holiday breaks. "I think Muffin and I would love that. It is a nice day and I haven't taken Muffin on a long walk yet."

Andrea heard some muffled talk and then Noah said, "Grandpa says we can be there in thirty minutes."

"Perfect. Muffin and I will see you then."

Andrea ended the call and looked at Muffin in silence for a few minutes. "Okay, girl. Walk first. Let's go see Noah on this pretty day."

As she changed to walking shoes, Andrea squelched her excited feelings over seeing Mark. *Remember, this is just a chance to let Noah play with Muffin. The boy's very excited to meet my new dog.*

Not quite sure she believed herself, Andrea put a leash on Muffin and practically skipped to the car.

"There she is." Noah cried from the bench facing the lake.

Before Mark could protest, the boy was running up to Andrea's car waving frantically to be seen.

It would be hard to miss the boy wearing a bright green shirt, jumping up and down on the sidewalk, Mark thought with a grin. He was surprised when Noah suggested they invite Andrea and Muffin for a walk, but thought it was a good idea since the boy had been cooped up with his sick little sister.

Eva had a cold and Mark had volunteered to take Noah for a few days since Kip was working long hours at the hospital to take time off for Christmas and Becka had enough to handle with a sick child.

Walking up to Andrea as she got out of her car, he smiled to see the small beagle bounce out and onto a giggling Noah.

As boy and dog started chasing each other, Mark extended his hand, "It's nice to see you, again."

"You too, Mr. Hastings."

"Mark, please."

"Andrea."

Unsure what to say next, they followed Noah and Muffin over to the lake to watch them play fetch with the ball Andrea brought. Mark sat next to her on a bench. "Noah mentioned you're not from Cartersville."

Turning to face him, Andrea struggled to focus on his words as she stared up into his eyes. *They're so striking. I feel he can read me too easily with his piercing blue stare.* "I'm from all over really. My dad was in the military and I married a man in the Marines. We were living in California when he passed unexpectedly in February of '09. I moved out here that November with my oldest son when his job transferred him to Atlanta."

"I'm sorry about your husband."

Moving a stray hair back, she smiled. "Thank you. It's been a few years now, and it's easier to look back and smile at the memories. It's hard when it comes out of the blue. No warning, no time to adjust."

"My father died in a car crash when I was nineteen. It was hard since I didn't get to see him. He was cremated and I regret I never got to speak to him one last time."

Putting her hand on his arm, Andrea squeezed gently, "I'm sorry, Mark."

With a wry grin, Mark patted her hand. "We weren't on the best of terms. He had a drinking problem and the accident was his fault. Thankfully, he didn't kill anyone else, but it was hard for my mom and me. We took things one day at a time, but honestly we felt more relief than pain at his loss."

"Nineteen is young to lose a parent, no matter how they act." Pausing a moment, Andrea hesitated before asking, "Did you start writing after that?"

Grinning, Mark winked, "People usually ask about my books first thing."

She blushed, "I don't mean to pry. I just thought with such a tragic event, it would alter how you see the world and bring about big changes..." Stammering, she gushed out, "Or at least that's what happened to me when James died. I started re-evaluating things and deciding what I needed to do for me. It's how I became a caterer."

Mark's mouth fell open. *It was after Dad died, I started writing! I married Maggie shortly after that and when Kip was born, the science fiction series was born, too! But it was those late nights right after Dad passed my writing style was developed and honed.*

Looking at Andrea with new eyes, he said, "You are a very wise woman."

Andrea blushed a deeper shade of red. "No, just experienced."

"Ahh, yes, progress not perfection... So... you're a caterer?"

Grinning, Andrea launched into the safe topic of how she met Bailey, who became a business partner and daughter. "It was amazing how everything worked out. Josh and Bales are two of the reasons I smile every day."

"Wow, God's timing..."

"It is perfect."

"Mrs. Andrea... do you want to toss the ball with us?"

"Let's both go," Mark said, standing to his feet. He reached out to help Andrea stand and was surprised to feel a spark after barely touching her arm.

She looked down at his hand, and stuttered, "Yes... let's go play with Noah."

After an hour of tossing the ball, dog and playmate were worn out. Both were laying on the grass watching the ducks on the pond. Taking a break, Andrea and Mark sat down on the bench discussing older science fiction authors and the change in the genre over the last ten years.

"Grandpa?"

Mark looked up at his grandson, almost forgetting he wasn't alone with Andrea in the park. "Yes, Noah?"

"What are we having for dinner tonight?"

Mark looked quickly at his watch. "We need to go to the grocery store actually, so I can fix something for the two of us." Chuckling, Mark turned to Andrea, "He's constantly asking about his next meal. You would think his parents and I starve him."

"My boys were like that, too!" Seeing Noah walking over to them, she added, "It must be a growing boy thing."

Noah sat between them as Mark explained Eva being sick, and Noah spending a few days with him. "I'll be taking him back tomorrow for Christmas Eve."

"Oh, if you two want to come, my daughter and son are having a little party tonight for my birthday."

"Birthday?" Noah and Mark cried out at the same time.

"Yes," Andrea blushed. *Lord, I've never blushed so much in my life. Not even when I was dating James.*

"Happy Birthday, Mrs. Andrea," Noah threw his arms around her.

Andrea smiled at Noah. "Since you invited me to your birthday party, it's only right, I should invite you to mine. It's just dinner and fun at my home. There will actually be kids. Laura's bringing her son, Brian. He's only about a year or two older than you."

Turning to his grandpa, Noah tugged on his arm. "Can we go, Grandpa? Pleeease?"

Andrea smiled, remembering her own sons begging for things the same way. When Mark looked at her, he saw the smile lighting up her face, and found himself agreeing. *I should be working harder to stay away from this special lady.*

"Here's my address. It's at seven." Andrea pulled out her notebook and wrote down quick directions.

"Noah, we need to get going if we're going to get a gift."

Andrea shook her head, "Oh, no. No gifts, please." Looking down at Noah, "I'd be happy just for you both to show up. I never told Josh my friend from PT was the grandson of Mark Lawson. He'll be thrilled to meet you." Blushing, she said apologetically, "He'll probably bring you all of his Kip books to have you autograph each of them. I need to warn you he has both the kid and adult series."

"I'd be happy to sign them," Mark helped Andrea to her feet feeling a shock up his arm. *Stop touching her. It just makes it harder to get her smile out of your head.*

Later, when he and Noah were deciding what to buy Andrea, Mark told himself once again to stop thinking about her, but it was hard with Noah singing her praises constantly. Every time Mark saw something in the store that reminded him of her, he'd have to start all over again with his litany. *You're not to be attracted to Andrea. You've had your chance. Stop thinking about her.*

"You look lovely, Mom."

"Thank you, honey," Andrea ran her hands down gray dress pants.

"Yes, Mom, the blue top really makes the gold in your brown eyes shine."

"Thank you, Bales. I enjoyed shopping with you the other day. This is one of the outfits I bought."

A twinkle in her eyes, Bailey said, "I remember." She sent a knowing look at Josh, "Any particular reason you're wearing it tonight? I thought I said when you bought it that it would be a knockout outfit."

Blushing, Andrea turned away with a quick no. *They don't have to know about the spark I feel near Mark whenever he's around.* Feeling the blush rising, she shrugged her shoulders. *It's just me crushing on a celebrity, it's not real at all.* Catching a glance of herself in the hallway mirror, she thought, *but it doesn't hurt to look like a knockout.*

Thankfully the doorbell rang, and any further conversation was halted. Andrea spent the next thirty minutes amazed at all of the people arriving to celebrate her birthday. *Little get together, my foot,* she thought watching Bailey help her greet even more party guests. *There must be over fifty people here!*

Bailey had gone all out, setting up a buffet in the catering kitchen along the large island with an extravagant taco bar including all of the fixings. People were helping themselves and then moving around the house to find a seat to chat.

Andrea found herself constantly surrounded by party goers, never having so many people wish her happy birthday before. She grinned looking out at the crowd. *I could get used to this.*

"Happy Birthday, Mrs. Andrea." A young voice said.

Andrea turned from talking to Carrie Quinn to see Noah. "Thank you, sweetie. I'm so glad you and your Grandpa could make it."

After saying a quick hello to Mark, she turned back to Noah. "Laura's son, Brian is here and I told him you were coming. Let's go find him. I think most of the bigger kids are in the den watching a movie while eating."

Showing them the buffet, she helped Noah fill a plate. Andrea tried to focus on the grandson and not the grandpa. *It doesn't help Mark even looks like a dashing writer with his chinos, oxford shirt, and sweater. He's turning heads of most of the women here, no matter what age they are!*

Walking into the den, she spied Brian sitting next to Muffin on the large sofa. Waving to the boy, she whispered to Mark, "Muffin's enjoying this party more than me. She's been getting all of the cuddles and food she can handle."

Brian came over with Muffin trailing behind, and Andrea smiled as she introduced the two boys. "Brian, this is my friend from physical therapy I was telling you about." Turning to Noah, she said, "This is the son of a good friend of mine. You're close in age and I think you have some interests in common."

Brian and Noah looked at each other and for a moment no one spoke. Andrea sent up a silent prayer, *Lord, please let them become friends. I think they need each other.*

Brian looked up at Mark for a moment before turning to Noah. "Is that your Grandpa?"

Noah nodded but didn't say anything.

"Your Grandpa writes Kip Saturn stories?!?" The awe in his voice evident over the noise from the movie.

Noah's face broke out in a huge grin, "Yeah! You like Kip, too?"

Brian shook his head vigorously, "Yeah. He's the best. I want a dog like Neptune."

"Me, too!" Moving closer to Brian, Noah asked, "Did you know he's writing a story based on me?"

Eyes shining bright with admiration, Brian cut his eyes to Mark before saying, "That's so cool." Waving at the TV, Brian asked, "Let's go watch the movie!"

Noah only nodded, before walking over to the couch. Both boys climbed on the sofa with Muffin between them, content to be petted by both boys. They began an animated conversation about sci-fi and Andrea sighed with relief. *I'm glad they hit it off.*

Mark whispered to her as they left the den, "I don't know if you noticed at his birthday party, but Noah doesn't have any close friends his own age. He's struggling to get to know anyone since we moved down here. He pretty much only likes space, aliens, and Kip Saturn."

"It's understandable considering who his grandpa is."

"Yes, but I don't want to handicap him from making friends."

Andrea stopped Mark in the hall. "Noah isn't handicapped. He just has specific interests, which happen to be very normal for a boy his age."

"Most kids are into movies and shows that his parents, understandably, don't allow him to watch and it makes things hard, but it's important for each of us to do the next right thing."

Andrea nodded, "I understand. I kept a sharp eye on what my boys saw. There was very little TV in their lives and more outside playtime, games, or anything to challenge their young minds. Noah's the same way, he knows quality when he sees it. I think you'll find God's timing is perfect because Brian could use a good friend, too."

"Oh?" Mark raised an eyebrow.

"Yes, his father was killed overseas. Army. It's been hard for Brian and his mother. He struggles to make friends, too. I think Noah and Brian will be good for each other."

Mark didn't speak but looked at her his gaze so intent, Andrea felt herself blushing again. After a moment, Mark said, "It shouldn't be let go and let God, but let go and let Andrea. You're a wise woman. I've said it before and I'll say it again."

Andrea stepped back and mumbled thank you without looking at him. Taking a breath, she said quickly while walking away, "Let me introduce you to my son, Josh. He's been asking about you for over an hour now. He's been worse than a kid."

Mark let her step back and followed her to the dining room. "I'd love to meet him."

"And remember you volunteered to sign all of Josh's books. He's got them lined up in the living room. He grabbed them all as soon as I told him you were coming."

He laughed, "Well, it's the least I can do for my biggest fan." He followed behind her, looking forward to meeting her oldest. Earlier, he felt a bit like Josh, anxiously waiting until it was time to leave for the birthday party, and he wouldn't admit who was more excited, him or Noah.

Mark's Journal Entry – December 23, 2013

Lord,

It's late, and it took forever for Noah to quiet down from the party and go to sleep. I'll be glad when school starts back because these late nights are cutting into my writing time. I do my best work late in the evenings and keeping up with his energy level all day wears this old man out. My editor's wondering when he'll get the first draft of my new series - I'm overdue. I can't remember a time I was late like this.

We attended Andrea's birthday party this evening and I'm glad Noah talked me into meeting her for a walk this morning. I never realized until we talked, how my dad's death influenced my desire to start writing. Andrea knew it before I did!

Andrea! Well, what can I say, except wow!

God, sometimes You have a quirky sense of humor - sending me the perfect woman, whom we both know I can't have. I wouldn't trade my short-lived marriage with Maggie for anything - I got Kip from that time. But lately, just between me and You, I have to wonder what life would be like if I could ask Andrea out.

I know You aren't cruel but at this moment... well, it's hard to see Your reason for putting this woman in my life. She's too good for me.

Her son reminds me so much of her. He's a great kid and I can see why she's proud of him. She wasn't kidding when she said he had every Kip novel, both the young adult and adult series. I autographed over thirty books tonight. I'm struggling to write this my hand's cramping so much. But I loved every minute!

The party, Andrea's friends and family, even when she opened gifts was fun. I learned so much about her by the gifts people chose, such well thought out presents for a kind woman. When Noah wanted to buy her a pretty notebook, I thought it would be too simple, but she loved it. Hugging my grandson like he'd bought her the moon. She put it in her purse right then after showing it off to friends and family.

Andrea. I tell myself I need to stay away from her, but it seems my plan keeps failing. Bailey, Andrea's new daughter-in-law invited the whole family over for a New Year's Eve party at their home. She wants to start a new family tradition and Noah's already excited to see Brian again. Andrea was right, he and Brian hit it off. You would think they've known each other for years instead of hours.

That reminds me, I met Laura Flowers before we left. The sweet woman wants me to give Becka her number to set up play dates for the boys. She's thrilled her son has a new friend, too!

Andrea was right. AGAIN. Lord, what were You thinking?!?

I've got to get to bed. Tomorrow's Christmas Eve and we've got family time. I need to schedule some time for writing in the morning. I'm falling behind and my publisher's getting anxious and truth be told, so am I.

Chapter Nine

"Hello, Andrea?"

"Yes, this is she."

"It's Mark, Mark Hastings."

"Oh, hello. How are you?"

"Good." Mark paused and Andrea wondered what was going on. *At least over the phone, he won't see me if I blush.*

"Actually, I'm having writer's block and thought a change of scenery is called for to help me get the creativity flowing again. I wanted to know if you would like to go to Atlanta with me and check out this Pink Pig ride I've heard so much about. I need to people watch and I know you mentioned wanting to do something the day after Christmas to give the newlyweds some time alone."

Smiling, because he remembered something she said to another lady in passing at her birthday party, Andrea said, "That sounds like fun. I haven't actually been. When would you like to go?"

"I can pick you up in thirty minutes. Does that work for you? I can give you longer if you need it."

"No, that's plenty of time." After Andrea hung up, she looked at her dog asleep on the sofa in her small living room. "Muffin, I'm going out with Mark and I feel like a school girl getting ready for a date."

Continuing to talk to the sleeping dog, Andrea frowned feeling a blush rise on her cheeks. "But this isn't a date. He just wants company and knows I wanted to get out of the house today..." Getting up to put on shoes, Andrea looked in the mirror and debated putting on a touch of makeup or not. "I'm being silly. We're just friends."

Leaving the sleeping dog, Andrea went in search of Bailey and Josh. She found them in the kitchen, lingering over pancakes.

Bailey looked up, fork in hand. "Hey, Mom. Want me to fix you a plate? There's plenty."

She started to rise, but Andrea waved her back down. "Thank you, but no. I'm actually leaving and wanted to know if you'd keep an eye on Muffin. I'm not sure how long I'll be gone."

Josh looked up from his plate, fork halfway to his mouth. "Leaving? You planning on coming back or have we already run you off?"

Snorting, Andrea waved. "Never, but Mark Hastings called and wants to go check out the Pink Pig ride in Buckhead."

"Mark?" Bailey smiled, hiding a wink at Josh. "Sounds like fun."

Andrea ignored the implication. "He's got writer's block and needs a change of scenery. I'm only going to keep him company."

Josh continued to finish his pancakes. "Well, make sure you don't break curfew and if he gets handsy, call me. I can take him out if need be."

"JOSHUA JAMES CABOT! We're only friends."

"Whatever you say, Mom. I've learned my lesson about meddling in your life." He kissed her cheek, before taking his plate to the dishwasher, saying over his shoulder, "Just know, I'm here if you need me."

"Josh, we're just friends."

"Okay, Mom."

"We are!" Andrea muttered, hands on her hips. *I can hear the disbelief his voice.*

"We believe you, Mom." Picking up the plate Josh put in the wrong spot, Bailey smiled at Andrea, while putting it in the right location. "We'll see you when you get back. Have fun."

Before Andrea could reply, the doorbell rang and she moved to pick up her purse. Over her shoulder, she called, "We're just friends, you two, just friends."

Andrea yanked open the door, muttering about ungrateful sons and stopped in her tracks when she saw Mark looking dreamy in a turtleneck and dark wash jeans. She was momentarily speechless until she saw the green convertible behind him in the driveway.

"Oh my gosh, that's a DB4 1960 Aston Martin," she exclaimed. "Oh, wow, it's a 2+2 drophead, too!"

Lord, she knows cars, too! Help me... Nodding, Mark held out his arm. "Yes, I bought it shortly after I sold my third novel and knew I had made it as an author. Growing up, granddad had an old beat up DB series he tinkered on for years trying to get working..." Helping her into the car, Mark walked around to other side and continued once he had settled in his seat., "It was my dream car as a little boy. Grandpa and I worked on that old clunker all the time. He died when I was seven and Grandma sold it." Remembering sitting in the ripped leather seat with his grandpa talking about life, Mark grew silent.

Andrea ran her hands over the leather, smiling like a teenage girl. "It's beautiful. My father loved old cars. He could never afford one, but he loved to look. We went to car shows a lot when I was little. It became our thing."

Turning the engine over, Mark grinned, "I know it's too cold to put the top down for the drive, but I thought it would still be fun for the ride to Atlanta."

Settling in the seat, Andrea gave a laugh when an Elvis song came out of the upgraded stereo system. Mark shrugged, "I only play the classics when I drive her. It seems only fitting."

"I understand." Andrea hummed along to the familiar song.

"I knew you would." Starting to drive, Mark asked, "Ready to go?"

Andrea nodded, excited for this unexpected adventure. *Just friends, Lord. We're just friends. Don't let me forget, I like being single and doing my own thing.*

"That was fun." Andrea turned with a big grin plastered on her face, "I'm glad we weren't the only adults riding."

Mark laughed, "Yes, I thought since I'm writing a new kid's series, I should be around children but didn't want to be a solo man riding the Pink Pig."

"That's why you invited me." She turned to hide her disappointment. *See, this isn't a date. I'm only here so he doesn't get arrested for stalking.*

Understanding dawning, she kept telling herself not to be upset. Turning her attention back to Mark, Andrea asked, "You said you were struggling with writer's block...?"

Mark put his arm around Andrea, leading her through the crowd in the mall as he talked. "Yes, the series I'm working on is based on Noah's name, Neurological Optimal Animatronic Humanoid."

"Yes, Noah told me that part. He's so excited you're creating a new storyline based on him, not just his dad."

He frowned, "I knew my young Kip stories had reached a natural stopping point and since I'd introduced Noah's namesake a few books ago... I thought this would be a great direction for a new kid's series."

"But?" Andrea could hear the frustration in his voice.

"I'm stuck," Mark whispered.

Andrea had to lean forward in the crowd to hear him. The day after Christmas, the mall was jammed packed with people taking advantage of year-end deals. Mark didn't continue but stopped in front of an ice cream kiosk and raised an eyebrow toward Andrea.

"Yes, please."

After ordering a butter pecan, Andrea tried to pay, but Mark waved her money away. "My treat for keeping me in such lovely company."

After getting his strawberry ice cream, he steered her toward an empty bench on the outskirts of the mall and they started eating, neither speaking. Andrea watched fascinated as families with young children walked by, young couples strolling arm in arm, and teenagers trying to look older and cooler.

I can see why Mark would want to come here, there's so much energy and mystery. These people all have a unique story. God, I see all of these people rushing around the day after Christmas and I'm reminded You sent Your Son for all of us. Please help Mark find the answers he's looking for to create the perfect story for Noah.

"My editor called this morning. I have a rough draft due by the end of March. Usually, I send him updates and teaser chapters... he's a big fan." Mark winked at Andrea, "But, I haven't sent him anything since the initial proposal months ago."

"So that's why you've started to panic a bit. How are you stuck? Plot? Themes?" Andrea asked, licking her ice cream cone.

Distracted by watching her, it took Mark a moment to focus on her words. "Um... Well, I've got the first part outlined, and I know how I want the first book to end. It's the middle I'm struggling to figure out. I need a good villain."

Andrea's golden eyes shined bright, "Yes, Dr. Mars was a great bad guy."

"Exactly!" Mark slapped his knee, "How do you top your first great villain?!?" Mark crunched down on his ice cream cone grateful Andrea understood his dilemma.

"Well, from what our Noah said, your main character, NOAH is a robot trying to find his place in a non-robot world." Eating her ice cream, she didn't look at Mark but continued thinking out loud, "Why not have multiple characters for your bad guy. You always explore deeper themes in your novels, explore bullying and acceptance for being different."

When Mark didn't say anything, Andrea looked up from her butter pecan. "I was just thinking out loud. I'm not a writer... I..."

"Andrea!" Mark slapped his forehead, "You're brilliant."

Andrea snorted, "Not really. You've got to stop saying that. I'll get a big head."

Mark leaned forward, grinning from ear to ear. "Never!" Reaching for her hand, he helped her stand. "I need to write some things down... all of the ideas are coming so fast I won't be able to get them down with just a pen and paper. I need to grab my laptop."

Smiling to see this grown man acting like an excited child, she asked, "Do you have your laptop with you?"

Mark turned, raising an eyebrow, "Of course. As a writer, I try to never leave home without it. I never know when I'm going to need to type something out."

"Would a coffee shop be a good place for you to write your ideas down at?"

"Umm... Yeees..." Mark drew out the word, unsure what Andrea was thinking.

"Perfect. I know just the place. Let's go!" She reached for his arm and started pulling him along at a brisk pace.

"But, Andrea," Mark tried to slow her down, "What will you do while I'm typing away. I'm not very chatty when I'm working. I could just type a few things out and…"

"Don't worry. I've got my new notebook from Noah I've been itching to write in. I've got a wedding in June to plan and several other events. I can keep myself busy, but when the muse hits you, I know you need to write. Don't worry."

"Okay, lead on," Mark followed, gripping Andrea's hand more firmly.

Hours later, Andrea laid in bed staring out the window petting a sleeping Muffin. *I can't sleep, Lord. I had such a fun day with Mark. I took him to the coffee shop on the river and we had the best time. We didn't get back home until after ten. Mark got so much writing done, he treated me to dinner for being his muse and for not complaining because we were at the coffee shop for over two hours with him typing away. He apologized while we were eating for being so quiet and leaving me alone after he had invited me to go out. I smiled and said not to worry.*

I don't think he realized he did talk to me, a lot! He would often ask my opinion on this or that, talking about different plot points and other stuff. It makes my heart happy to know he values my ideas. I think he was a little shocked when I suggested one of the villains have a snot problem, but he needs to remember I did raise two boys! Dinner was wonderful too because we talked about so many things besides his writing. We've read a lot of the same books, and watched many of the same movies…

Rolling over, cuddling Muffin, Andrea thought about James. They two of them had rarely spent time together just sitting or with small talk. Her husband was always on the go, needing to be moving or doing something. Long vacations were hard because he hated to be stuck in a car for the lengthy ride to their destination. *We never would have gone to a coffee shop just to sit and talk, and enjoy spending time together just the two of us.*

Frowning, she petted a sleeping Muffin, "I shouldn't compare the two. They are very different men." Muffin lifted her head to rest on Andrea's arm. "I can't believe I'm… well, none of that matters… Mark and I are only friends. And I happen to like being single, so it doesn't matter he only invited me to keep him company and nothing more."

Snuggling deeper under the covers, Andrea said her prayers and fell asleep thinking about plans for the New Year's Eve party she was organizing with Bailey. She ignored the happiness she felt at the thought of seeing Mark again so soon.

Chapter Ten

"Is he here, yet?"

Andrea looked up from filling glasses with ice to see Noah's expectant face. She ruffled his hair, "Soon. Brian's other grandparents have been visiting, but they were supposed to leave today."

Noah looked at his feet. "Oh." Running his foot back and forth along the island. "Ok."

As he walked off, Andrea chuckled to herself. *That's the third time he's asked about Brian, and Noah would laugh to know Brian was the same way at church the other day, making sure he would be here tonight.* Looking at her watch, she saw it was almost nine. *Everyone should be here soon. I better check on the others.*

Walking out the back-kitchen door, she grabbed her coat off the back of a chair and stepped outside. She saw a group of men standing around a large bonfire, or at least the start of one.

"Maybe we should pile the sticks like this..."

"No, that will let the fire burn too quickly." Josh interrupted Cole.

"But what if..."

"How about..."

Andrea smiled to herself, watching her son and his friends discussing the best way to build a fire to roast marshmallows later. *I might need to step in or they'll never get the fire ready.*

Before she could speak up, a deep calming voice said, "Gentlemen, why don't we create a small pile of sticks and add more as we need to."

Steven piped up, "Good idea, Mark. We don't need to start it yet, anyway."

Andrea stepped back when she saw Mark come around the side of the barn with an armload of branches in hand. She watched the group of six men make the pile exactly the way Mark suggested, and as her son clapped Mark on the back, she was glad to see Josh had finally relaxed around him. *The hero worship on my birthday probably overwhelmed poor Mark. Josh could hardly speak the first time they met. His face turned red, and he struggled to think of simple words.*

"Hi, Mom. Come to check on our progress?"

"Looks good. Grace and Laura will bring the kids out in a bit for s'mores."

Mark moved closer to stand right next to Andrea. "Has Noah been asking about Brian?"

Andrea blushed, before stuttering out, "A few times." *Good Lord, I've got a crush, not just Joshua!*

Clearing her throat, she said, "I'm glad they've hit it off so well."

When the others began to walk back inside, Mark motioned for Andrea to proceed him. Glad it was dark to hide any blushing, Andrea took only a few steps before her foot went into a hole and she stumbled. Strong arms grabbed her around the waist, keeping her from falling on her face. "Thank you." *Lord, don't let him think I did that on purpose.*

Mark kept his arm around her, gently guiding her back to the kitchen door. Andrea found herself safe and content in his arms, and told herself to stop, even though suddenly she felt it was a bit too warm outside.

Holding the door, Andrea stepped inside first to see most everyone had arrived and were in the kitchen getting snacks. Turning to Mark, she said another quick thank you, before rushing to help with drinks.

"Sorry, we're late, Andrea. My mother-in-law wouldn't leave for the longest time."

Andrea looked up to see a willowy brunette walking toward her looking a little frazzled with her hair down and windblown. "It's fine, Laura. It's not a formal party, people are coming and going like crazy."

Looking at the large group mingling in the kitchen, Andrea chuckled, "I think Bailey invited half the town."

Hearing her name, Bailey walked over. "Of course, I did, Mom. What's the point of having a huge house for entertaining if we don't use it?!?" Pushing a few strands of short, red hair back from her face, Bailey smiled, "Plus, I wanted to see your new boyfriend a bit more."

Andrea, feeling her face going scarlet, turned to fill more glasses with ice. "Mark is not my boyfriend. He's just a friend. His grandson and Laura's son, Brian have become best buddies."

Bailey only nodded but winked at Laura. "Of course."

Laura began to help fill glasses with water and tea. "Noah's been a godsend. He and Brian have become best friends in such a short amount of time. My son has struggled to be the little boy he is since his father died."

Bailey put her arm around Laura. "I know it's been hard for all of you. I'm glad they found each other."

Wiping away a tear, Laura murmured, "It's all because of Andrea. She introduced them at her birthday party." Tears started to fall quickly and Laura whispered, "Excuse me," already bolting from the room.

Bailey caught Andrea's eye before the older woman put a glass down to go find Laura. Bailey said as she followed after her, "Tell her we're praying and let me know if I can do anything."

Andrea only nodded, seeing Bailey took up her position filling glasses. Rounding the corner, she saw there was a line to the bathroom, but couldn't find Laura anywhere. *Lord, where could she have gone?*

Hearing sobbing, Andrea made her way to her little cottage and found Laura sitting on her couch crying. "Laura, honey, what is wrong?"

Taking the petite woman into her arms, Andrea rubbed her back. "Tell me what's going on and we'll figure out how to solve this or pray for God to take care of it."

"Penny told me tonight she and her husband are moving down in July. If they haven't found a place by then, she said... they'll... they..." Laura couldn't continue, she was so upset, she struggled to breathe.

"Laura, deep breath. I promise it will be okay."

After helping the woman calm down, Andrea asked after a few quiet moments, "Now, what did Penny tell you that has you so upset?"

"She told me she and Bob would move in with us. We have a spare bedroom in the apartment and it would be perfect." Eyes wild, Laura cried, "I can't have that woman living with me. She criticizes everything I do and plus, well, she talks about what a saint her son was and how she wants MY SON to grow up to be just like him."

Patting the woman's pale hand, Andrea asked quietly, "They don't know he was abusive toward you?"

Laura shrugged, "No, no one does. I've only talked to you and one other woman about it. A friend I knew in high school."

Tears filling her blue-gray eyes once again, Laura whispered, "I don't know what to do. I don't want them around Brian all the time. They aren't Christians and Bob has a temper. I don't know what would happen if they knew about Blake. I'm trying to put what he did behind me and move on, but it's so hard when they talk about how wonderful he was and how they miss him so."

Laura wiped away a tear. "I was so relieved when he died. I didn't believe it was really over for a long time, every door slam or car pulling into the driveway I thought was him, but once it sunk in it was over, it was like I could breathe for the first time in years." Turning to Andrea, Laura asked softly, "Is that wrong?"

"No, sweetie, it isn't."

Sighing, Laura leaned back, "I don't know what to do. I keep praying they find a house, but..."

With a twinkle in her eye, Andrea said, "I had a thought about this exact problem. You see, Bailey has moved out of her rental place and I know you had been looking for a home for you and Brian before this happened and well..."

"The Adams' rental house?"

"Yes, have you been there?"

"Once for Bailey's wedding shower. It's beautiful."

"And perfect for you and Brian. It has two bedrooms each with its own bathroom and NO EXTRA guestrooms."

"It is very nice, but it's another rental."

"Well, I talked to Noelle and Michael, they would actually like to sell the place."

Laura's eyes brightened as a large smile crossed her face, "Really? It's a wonderful house. A big backyard, an amazing kitchen..." Before she continued, Laura started to laugh softly.

"What's so funny?"

"I won't be able to tell Brian no about getting a dog anymore. My biggest reason for no is we're in a rental. The Adams' place even has a fenced in yard!"

"Perfect for a young boy."

Laura nodded, "Yes, and it would put us closer to not only you but Noah's family as well."

"Yes, they'll be in the same school now."

Leaning forward, Laura hugged Andrea. "I can't tell you how much you have meant to me the last few months. You've been such a blessing."

"Oh sweetie, I'm honored to be your friend. I think of you as part of the family."

"Thank you." Wiping her eyes, Laura looked at the clock, "We should head back to the party, everyone's going to wonder where you are, especially your boyfriend."

"Oh no, not you, too!"

"Andrea, I might be a widow with a terrible marriage in my past but I still recognize when a man's falling for a woman."

Andrea waved her hand at Laura. "Please, we're only friends. Just similar in age, surrounded by all you young people is all."

Laura rolled her eyes, "Andrea, my friend, I'm a terrible judge of character, but that man spends all his time watching you."

Andrea felt herself blushing again, but shook her head, "No. He doesn't. Plus, I can't date." Snorting, she huffed, "Who has the time with a catering business to run and keeping up with all of you? I enjoy my life, my freedom, and my independence."

Standing up, Laura smiled wistfully, "I understand all of that, especially freedom and independence, but even after all I've been through with Blake, there are times, rare though they are, when I wish I had someone special. Someone to look at me the way Mark looks at you."

"Really, Laura? You've never shown any interest in dating, quite the opposite in fact."

Smoothing out her skirt, staring at her cowboy boots, Laura sighed, "Yes, it's true. I'd probably start running if someone actually showed me any interest, the fear is there and I don't think it will ever go away, but raising a boy on my own, sometimes I wish…"

"Mom, are you coming back out? I can't find the lighter."

Sighing, Andrea called out, "Yes, Josh. It's in the box by the fireplace. I'll be out in a moment."

She laughed turning to Laura. "Even with big boys, it would be nice to have someone, but I promise you, Mark and I are just friends. Nothing more."

Any more talk with Laura was put on hold when the two women went back out to join the party. The house was packed with adults and kids until Grace, Carrie, and a few other parents took the kids outside to enjoy the s'mores bar Bailey had set up earlier. A few of the adults went out to enjoy them too, even without kids of their own.

Sharon walked up to Andrea and stopped her. "Is Bailey around? I want to get her recipe for that chocolate dip thing. It's amazing."

"It is divine."

"One of the many things I love about Bailey is she happily shares recipes. When I worked as a manager for a restaurant in Chicago, chefs kept their recipes a treasured secret."

"You're from Chicago?"

Andrea and Sharon turned to Mark who had walked inside to warm up his hands. "Hi, I'm Mark Hastings. I was born and raised in Chicago."

Sharon smiled, extending her hand, "Yes, I grew up there. This March, I will have been in Cartersville for two years."

"What part of Chicago?"

Andrea left Sharon and Mark to compare old stomping grounds and went in search of Bailey to let her know Sharon wanted the recipe for the chocolate dip.

Bailey's right, we will have to make this an annual event. Andrea spent the next few hours talking with friends, holding baby Grace Anne, and enjoying herself immensely.

Hours later after looking at her watch, she saw it was getting close to midnight and wanted to make sure she had enough matches for the sparklers everyone was lighting to ring in the New Year. Viviane had already gone outside to set up her camera to take pictures of the event.

Walking into the kitchen, Andrea moved to the deep pantry to grab the extra matches Bailey kept in a labeled container. Chuckling to see Bailey's organized pantry in comparison to her messy habits, Andrea thought, *Josh and Bales are still learning to deal with their different levels of neatness. It's been entertaining to watch.*

"Andrea?"

Andrea turned around to see Mark standing close in the suddenly tiny pantry. "Did you need something, Mark?" *Good Lord, do I have to sound so breathless?*

Mark started to speak but froze to see Andrea in the dim light, a slight blush across her cheeks. *I've spent the entire night telling everyone we're just friends, but I can't deny how much I want to kiss her right at this very moment.*

Frozen, Andrea couldn't move and after only a moment's hesitation, Mark leaned forward. Kissing her softly, Mark thought, *honestly Lord, we both know I've wanted to kiss her since the day we first met at Noah's birthday party.*

Time stood still and Andrea felt herself giving into the kiss. She wrapped her arms around Mark as he put his arms around her waist. *This is nice,* Andrea thought after a few moments.

Suddenly breaking free, each looked in the other's eye, unsure of how to react. Mark started to stutter, but no coherent words came out.

Andrea, trying to hide her blushing, stammered out, "I need to see if Bale's needs me."

As Andrea rushed off, Mark watched her leave, feeling very alone and cold in the empty pantry. *Lord, what have I done? I can't see Andrea as anything more than a friend! I know I can't make anything work with her.*

"Andrea," Carrie called coming around the kitchen corner.

Andrea jerked her head up to see Carrie and Aiden coming in the back door looking for her. "We want you for some pictures." Seeing her flushed face, Carrie asked, "Are you okay?"

"Yes, I'm fine. Just ran inside a moment to grab more matches."

"Well, let's hurry. It's almost midnight and we don't want to miss out." Aiden held the door open for the ladies.

Andrea was grateful for the interruption. It gave her a chance to come to her senses. *What was I thinking, Lord? I was practically making out with a man in my pantry!?! Good grief, I'm in my fifties!*

Mark's Journal Entry – January 1, 2014

Lord,

This isn't how I wanted to spend the first day of the New Year. It's almost the end of the day and I've gotten nothing done on my book today. I had set time for outlining the rest of the novel for Noah's story and I'm stuck. All I can think about is Andrea last night. After our kiss, we avoided each other for the short time the party lasted after sparklers and pictures.

I was actually jealous of my eight-year-old grandson because at midnight Noah ran to her for a New Year's kiss and Andrea laughing kissed him and didn't run away!

What's wrong with me? I've told myself nothing can happen with Andrea. The AA meeting, I attended this morning was just another reminder. Since I hit my twenty-year mark, I only attend once a month, but this morning I felt I needed a reminder of why Andrea and I can't be anything more than friends.

Lord, please help me remember that!

Chapter Eleven

Cuddled under the covers, Andrea ignored Muffin licking her feet as an encouragement to get up. *I know I need to walk Muffin and then get ready for church, but I'm not quite ready to face the day.* Pulling out her Bible, Andrea turned to Philippians chapter four and started reading. Absent-mindedly petting Muffin, she found herself re-reading verses four through seven. "Rejoice in the Lord always. I will say it again: Rejoice! Let your gentleness be evident to all. The Lord is near. Do not be anxious about anything, but in every situation, by prayer and petition, with thanksgiving, present your requests to God. And the peace of God, which transcends all understanding, will guard your hearts and minds in Christ Jesus."

"Lord, I've really been struggling since Mark and I kissed on New Year's Eve." Continuing to pet Muffin, Andrea closed her Bible and prayed, "I need to remember I'm in my fifties and not a teenage girl with a crush. Please help me to see Mark Hastings as only a friend and nothing more. I like my life right now and a man in it would just be confusing. This is just a silly crush and I need to move past it."

Before Andrea could continue, her phone rang, and she told herself to squash the hope it was Mark calling. They had not seen each other since the kiss and while she didn't know how to react, she missed their friendship. Seeing it was an unknown number, Andrea answered, "Hello?"

"Hello, Andrea. It's Lauren Blake."

"Hi, Lauren. How are you?"

"I'm good. I wanted to see if you and Bailey would be able to meet with Hillary this afternoon instead of next Saturday. Daniel has a karate event that day and the whole family will be there to support him."

"What time? I can check with Bailey, but I'm sure it will be fine."

"Would three work? We can meet wherever is convenient for you both. Hillary and Luke will be driving up with the kids, but Alex can watch them if need be."

"Why don't you all come over to our house? We've got plenty of room for the kids to play and Josh can help Alex keep an eye on them while we plan Hillary's wedding in April."

"Perfect. I'll see you then."

Rubbing Muffin's belly, Andrea set the phone down. "Little girl, I've got to get up now. I need to get to church to talk to Bailey. They left early this morning to help Cole with something."

Andrea threw off the covers and rushed to get dressed. She chuckled to see Muffin stayed in bed sleeping. *Didn't she want to get up earlier? Or was she just trying to get me up so the alarm would quit going off every nine minutes and disturb her beauty sleep?!?*

She didn't stop to wonder about her silly dog but got dressed in record time. When she finally made it to Grace's Sunday School classroom, Andrea was glad to see Bailey was there with Grace and Viviane chatting before the lesson started. Walking over to hug the ladies, Andrea turned to Bailey. "Lauren Blake called me this morning, Bales. They need to move their appointment to three this afternoon. Does that work for you?"

Bailey finished her bite of muffin, before replying with a smile. "That's perfect."

"How is Lauren?" Grace asked, enjoying Bailey's famous peanut butter honey muffins people jokingly say won her a husband.

Viviane's eyes twinkled, "Very well. I didn't get a chance to tell you, but a few days before the wedding, she came over to Cole's house and apologized to us both."

Grace's mouth dropped open, "What?"

"Yes," Viviane wiped her hands with a napkin, before continuing. "It seems she has really changed after she had the big fight with Hillary over Luke and his kids.

Lauren's become a kind, sweet woman of God and I've been truly blessed to call her a friend. She and her husband are more involved with the kids' ministry at church. She laughingly says she needs the practice with three instant grandkids."

Tears in her green eyes, Grace smiled, "That's wonderful. Hillary told me she and her mother have really strengthened their mother-daughter relationship. It's the best it's ever been."

Andrea snagged a muffin. "It says in Psalms to create in me a clean heart and renew a right spirit within me. It's something that needs to be done constantly, and as adults, I think we forget we need to be renewed daily."

Viviane nodded while finishing the last bite. "Lauren mentioned God spoke to her and told her straight out she had forgotten her first love. She admitted to Cole and me, she was more focused on actions and looking right, than having a right heart."

"It's something we all forget at times," Grace rose with her Bible in hand. "Which is why we have things like Sunday School to remind us."

Bailey laughed, "That's Grace's subtle way of letting us know it's time class started."

Grace winked at the ladies while calling everyone's attention to the front.

Andrea listened with one ear but kept thinking of her verse this morning before Lauren called. *I was anxious about the Mark situation, but honestly, I won't see him that often. There are no more events for us to run into each other at and it's probably for the best.*

Telling herself to be content, she focused on the lesson. After the teaching was over, Andrea helped the ladies clean up before the group made their way downstairs for the service. Andrea was focused on Bailey talking about ideas for Hillary's wedding when she saw a flash of blue come flying at her.

"Mrs. Andrea! There you are!"

Andrea looked up to see Noah flying toward her with his parents and grandfather right behind him.

"Hello, Noah! I didn't know you were coming!"

Hugging the boy, she looked over at Kip and Becka smiling at her. Becka waved. "We've been going to a church further south, but Noah kept begging us to try this church because he says it's where Brian and Mrs. Andrea go."

Kip laughed, "It was an easier drive that's for sure."

"I'm glad you could attend. We do have a great children's ministry. Carrie Quinn is amazing and the teaching for adults is wonderful."

Becka came forward for a hug. "The congregation has been warm and welcoming, too. I enjoyed our couples' class this morning." Whispering, she said to Andrea, "I think more than one guy wanted to see you today."

Andrea blushed but turned to Noah. "Are you on your way to Children's church? Brian's already there. I saw his mother this morning."

Noah nodded, and took Andrea's hand, "Can you walk me there?"

"Of course." She turned to Bailey, "Save me a seat?"

"Sure, Mom."

Andrea forced herself to focus on Noah and not his grandfather. She was grateful it was only the two of them walking to children's area. *Lord, didn't we just establish it was best if I didn't see Mark Lawson Hastings, anymore?!?*

After dropping off Noah, Andrea made her way back to the sanctuary to grab the seat Bailey would have saved for her. She was glad Noah's family was going to attend the church. It was a joy to see Noah and Brian excited to see each other this morning. *Those two boys have a friendship like David and Jonathan in the Bible instant, real, and deep.*

The service had started when she arrived and waving to a few people as she made her way to the front, she couldn't see very well with everyone standing and singing for worship. Sliding into the pew, she smiled at Bailey before turning to her right and saw Mark was the one sitting next to her. *Oh dear!*

Hours later, Andrea didn't think she would be able to focus when Hillary and her family came to discuss the wedding details for the April wedding. Splashing water on her face in the powder room, she looked in the mirror. She whispered, because she didn't want Josh or Bailey to overhear. "Andrea Cora Cabot, you stop this right now! It's only a silly crush, hero fascination and it means nothing. You two didn't even speak to each other today and you were beside each other on the same pew all morning and even sat together at lunch. Just because Noah's family asked Bailey, Josh and I to join them after church doesn't mean you have to obsess over the silver-headed fox."

She put the towel away and sighed in the mirror. "I miss being able to talk to him but it's only because it was nice having a friend close to my age... it's been weeks and we still don't even look at each other, which only proves we aren't meant to be anything more than acquaintances. Don't forget that!"

A doorbell sounded through the front of the house and Andrea left the bathroom to let the guests inside. Bailey and Josh were gathering supplies for Hillary's soon to be stepchildren to have things to do.

Opening the door, Andrea smiled at the growing family. "Come in, it's cold."

"Thank you, Andrea." Lauren Blake smiled holding baby Camila in her arms, while ushering Daniel into the house.

A tall, blonde young woman came in with a diaper bag and two kids' backpacks. "Thank you for being able to meet with us on such late notice. We just found out about Daniel's belt ceremony and since it's his first we're making it a big deal."

"Yes, I'm going to be a niña." A young boy with dark hair and chocolate brown eyes showed off a smile with a missing front tooth.

Laughing, a tall, muscled man walked in carrying a portable playpen, "Daniel, it's a ninja. Niña in Spanish means girl."

Daniel made a gagging sound, "Eww. Gross."

After everyone finished laughing, Luke set up the playpen, "Hi, Andrea. I'm Luke Toledo and this is my crazy crew."

"Our crazy crew, son."

Andrea looked behind Luke to see an older gentleman with graying hair carrying a dark-haired little girl. "We're going to be officially family soon so you might as well claim all of us." Kissing the little girl with pigtails, before setting her down, he took the diaper bag from Hillary. "We already act like family; this wedding and adoption is just to make it official."

Waving at Andrea, Alex set up the playpen in the living room.

After Lauren put Camilla in the playpen as she looked at her new family. "That's for sure. The Toledo, Blake, and Diego families celebrate every chance we get."

Andrea knew Luke's recently adopted nieces and nephew were doing better since last summer when Luke's sister died of a drug overdose. Luke and Hillary's love story had brought Andrea to tears when she first heard it.

God works in mysterious ways, Hillary being their nanny for that first difficult summer changed everything in the new family's lives. God knew Hillary would be the perfect nanny, being a teacher and understanding Spanish, since Luke's sister mostly spoke to them in Spanish.

Bailey and Josh came down the front stairs and after introductions and hugs, Andrea said, "The kids can spend time in the living room and I thought the planning committee could meet in the dining room so we can spread out on the large table."

"That's perfect, Andrea." Turning to her husband, Lauren kissed Alex. "Let's us know when you're ready to surrender."

"Never." Alex winked at her, before turning to Josh. "The two of us can handle three little kids."

Josh looked a little unsure, but Alex clapped him on the back and said quietly, "You'll need the practice now you're married."

Sending a panicked look at Bailey, Josh squatted down to pick up the toy Daniel handed him. Bailey mouthed, "You'll be fine," before leading Hillary, Luke, and Lauren to the dining area where they had set up everything.

Andrea asked, "Does anyone want anything? Coffee, tea?"

Hillary's smile grew large, "I'd love some tea. We were running late today and I've only had two cups."

"And in Hillary's world, that's like ten below normal."

"Luke!" Hillary and Lauren cried.

Smiling, a twinkle in his eyes, he put his arm around his fiancée. "But that's one of the many reasons I love her."

"You'd better, Mister Toledo."

Bailey showed Hillary the tea options in the kitchen, while Lauren and Luke talked to Andrea. Luke said, "Hillary wants a low-key wedding."

Lauren nodded, "And I'm honoring her wishes. She wants a simple, short ceremony because of the kids."

"... And because the two of us don't like being the center of attention."

Lauren smiled at her future son-in-law and continued, "Then a fun reception, simple but tasteful which fits my daughter perfectly."

Hillary walked back into the dining room with a beautiful smile, "Thank you, Mom." Sitting by her mother, Hillary hugged her. "It means so much to me that you're going along with all of our wishes."

Tears in her eyes, Lauren said, "I realized the extravagant wedding I've had in mind isn't suited to you and I have learned what you want is wonderful and perfect."

Hillary brushed tears away but beamed. "Well, then let's plan this wedding. We have only so long before the kids are going to tire out."

Luke kissed Hillary, before replying, "That's true."

Andrea pulled out the notebook Noah gave her for her birthday and asked, "Okay, Hillary and Luke. What are your thoughts?"

"Simple!" They both said in unison.

After everyone laughed, the group got down to business planning the wedding. Later, after they all left, Andrea thought of the sweet couple and all they had gone through to get where they are now. *Lord, I know they're meant to be together and raise those sweet kids. Daniel and Magda adore each of them and already think of them as Mom and Dad. It's so sweet. When the kids lost their mother to a drug overdose, I know Luke must have thought life was over. But, Lord, You had a good plan for all of them, even Hillary.*

Thinking about losing her husband five years ago next month, Andrea thought, *I believed life was over for me then – dead and gone, but You renewed my purpose in life and even brought us, Bailey. She was an unexpected blessing, a daughter and wife for the Cabot family!*

<u>Mark's Journal Entry – January 20, 2014</u>

Lord,

I haven't been able to write a single word in weeks. I don't know what's wrong with me. I've never had writer's block like this before. What happened? I had so many ideas in December and just a few weeks later, it's... well it's... all gone. I don't have amnesia so what's the problem?

While we're discussing problems, can we talk about how Andrea keeps showing up wherever I'm at? It's like the world's trying to throw us together. How many times do we have to tell people we're just friends? I swear Kip, Becka, AND Noah are creating "chance" meetings for the two of us like we'd signed up for some dating website.

I've tried everything to get past my writer's block but nothing is working. I find myself spending too much of my writing time thinking about the kiss on New Year's Eve. What was I thinking?!?

Lord, I could really use some help down here!

... Please don't let Andrea be the reason I can't write anymore...

Chapter Twelve

"Noah, don't forget your bedtime is nine on Friday nights. I've already reminded your grandfather, but I'm telling you, NO staying up late! Just because it isn't a school night, doesn't mean you get to stay up until eleven."

"Mooom!"

"I'm not kidding, Noah Lawson Hastings. We've got errands to run tomorrow and I don't want you falling asleep on me. You need new shoes."

"I hate shopping." Noah dragged his feet over the wooden kitchen floor, ignoring the fact his tennis shoes were starting to feel too tight. *But I don't want to waste a Saturday buying shoes when I could be playing with Grandpa. I haven't seen him in forever and I wanna go to the park tomorrow.*

"Son," Kip said looking up from the book he was reading at the kitchen island. "Shopping for clothes is a necessity until you're grown and can just order the same size online and have it shipped to your door."

"If I were Kip Saturn, I have a space suit that just grew with me."

"Boy, do I wish! It would save a lot of money. This is the second time in a year we've had to buy you new shoes and it's only February." Becka kissed her oldest, she turned to Kip. "I'm going change Eva before Mark arrives to babysit the kids tonight."

She and Kip had a date night for Valentine's Day with their new Sunday School class. A special dinner catered by Taste & See along with games were planned for the evening. *I'm looking forward to a romantic evening with my husband. With the crazy hours we've both been working lately, I feel like we haven't been together without kids in ages.*

Kip stood up to put away his book and ruffled his son's hair. *He is so much like his grandfather. Dad hasn't stepped into a clothing store in years. He orders online and has it shipped to him because he detests shopping so much. That must be where Noah gets his aversion from.*

"I'm here." A deep voice called from the living room.

"Grandpa!" Noah shouted, running into the living room to hug his grandfather. "I haven't seen you much lately."

Mark grunted, and carried Noah into the kitchen. Seeing his son, his grumpy mood softened a little. *Whatever I've done, it's good to see Kip's happy family. I must have done something right, Lord.*

"When do you need to head out, Kip?"

Kip grabbed his keys off the counter. "Soon. Becka's changing the baby and then we'll be leaving. We should be back by ten, ten-thirty at the latest. She wanted me to remind you Noah's bedtime is nine but it will give you time to write after the kids go to bed." *He looks awful, like he hasn't slept in days.*

Noticing his father's grimace at the word writing, Kip continued, "You must be writing up a storm because we haven't seen much of you in weeks."

Before Mark could reply, Becka walked back in and Kip let out a low whistle, "Who is this enchanting woman I'm taking out this evening?"

Becka's face brightened and she did a small twirl in the kitchen showing the sparkling black dress she had bought the other day. "I've already taken care of Eva. She's napping, and I just wanted a chance to put on something nice for this dinner Mark's girlfriend is catering."

"She IS NOT my girlfriend."

Everyone turned to face Mark, shocked at his loud, gruff tone. Seeing the look on their faces, Mark cleared his throat, "I'm sorry. I'm struggling with writer's block for the first time in my writing career and it has me a little bit on edge. But..."

Looking Kip and Becka in the eye, he said forcefully, "Andrea Cabot and I are NOT dating. I only see her at church and events with Noah."

Becka eyed him. *That's the problem! It isn't the writer's block - that's only a symptom.*

Mark didn't say anymore but marched to the living room to plug in his laptop.

Kip cleared his throat, "We need to leave, honey. You look beautiful and I want to show you off to all our new Sunday School friends. They need to see I married the most beautiful woman in the room."

Becka kissed Kip, before turning to Noah. She gave him her mom stare as she said firmly, "Bedtime is nine, young man."

"I know, Mom." Noah sighed, but ran up to her for a hug. "You do look pretty."

Tears in her eyes, Becka hugged him. "Thank you, sweetie. You're just as charming as your father."

After hugs and kisses, Kip and Becka left for their dinner talking about Mark's strange behavior along the way. Pulling into Andrea's driveway, Kip parked but didn't get out of the car. "I don't know what's wrong with dad!"

"I do," Becka chuckled.

"What?"

"He's in love with Andrea Cabot."

"What? Are you crazy?" He turned in his seat to look at his wife to see if she was kidding him.

"Love of my life, you are too left-brained sometimes. He loves her and he's struggling with it for some reason."

Is she right? Kip didn't say anything for a moment. "But he's never dated after he and my mom divorced. Not once! I know women were interested, but he never did anything about it that I know of growing up."

"So, that doesn't mean he doesn't want to now! Andrea's a wonderful, smart, and lovely woman. They'd be perfect for each other."

"Are you sure?" Kip shook his head, "No, I think you're wrong about this. They don't know each other that well. Besides, I don't think they've talked much outside of church when we all sit together."

"Oh, I'm sure all right. That's the reason for his writer's block, too. Remember when they first met and he was dancing for joy over the ideas about the NOAH story?"

"Yes, but that was the book NOT Andrea."

"They are linked." She kissed his cheek, "You'll see."

"But what about Andrea? How does she feel about all of this?"

Becka frowned. "That I don't know."

Seeing movement on the porch, Kip unlocked the car. "Well, we'll soon see. That's Andrea waving us inside."

Touching his wife's arm, he said quickly, "Wait there. I want to open the door for you and personally escort the prettiest lady inside."

As Kip walked around, Becka watched Andrea. *Lord, if these two are meant to be together, please work it out. My father-in-law can be a stubborn man sometimes.*

All thoughts of her father-in-law were forgotten as Becka took Kip's outstretched arm and looked forward to a fun evening.

Kip turned off the lights in the kitchen before grabbing his phone to check for any messages from the hospital. It was almost midnight and he was tired but had enjoyed the romantic evening out with his wife. Andrea was an excellent hostess and the class wanted to make the Valentine's dinner a reoccurring event. The games the woman had thought of were actually fun and most of the husbands enjoyed the evening, not just the wives.

Making sure the house was locked and all the lights were off, he nearly missed the quiet footsteps on the wood floor. "Noah? What are you doing up?"

Noah stood in the hallway, and Kip could barely make out his son's face but could see him in his Spiderman pajamas. "Are you okay, son? Are you sick? You'd better have a fever if you're planning on trying to get out of shoe shopping tomorrow. Your mother is determined you're getting new shoes."

"Dad?"

"Yes?" Kip could hear the tears in his little voice. He moved closer, "What's wrong, Noah?"

"What's the matter..." A big, hiccup from the boy was followed by, "What's wrong with Grandpa?"

Kip reached down to pick up Noah. *I won't be able to do this much longer. He's getting so big.* Carrying him back into the darkened living room, Kip settled him on the sofa. "What happened tonight?"

Burying his face in his dad's shoulder, Noah words were muffled. "He was grumpy. Not like himself at all. I asked him if I could read the next chapters of the book, but he just said it wasn't ready." Looking up at his dad, Noah said in a shocked tone, "Dad, he always lets me read his stuff before it's finished!"

Kip could see the tears in his son's blue eyes with the moonlight streaming in from the window and his heart ached for his little boy.

"He doesn't laugh anymore or make up silly stories." Snuffling, Noah wiped his nose on his sleeve. "He wouldn't play with me or Eva tonight, because he had work to do, but then... he... he just stared at the screen the whole night. He didn't type a single word."

"I know, son. Sometimes adults, especially men, don't handle their emotions well."

"Uh? I don't get it. What do emotions have to do with Grandpa not being much fun?"

"Yeah, well, I think Grandpa's struggling to write his next book and it's making him a bit gruff with everyone. You know he's never struggled to write before."

"Is it because of Mrs. Andrea?"

Kip looked at his son in shock. *He thinks so, too! Good grief, I'm not really THAT dense, am I, Lord?*

Nodding, Kip decided he needed to pay more attention to his dad and non-girlfriend. "Yeah, I think you and Mom are right and Grandpa doesn't know how to deal with his feelings for Mrs. Andrea. You know he's been alone since he and Grandma Mags divorced when I was a little guy not much older than you."

Noah was quiet for a moment, "That's a long time."

Kip chuckled and ruffled the boy's hair. "Thanks, bud, but I'm not THAT old."

"I just wish I knew what to do to help him," Noah huffed.

"Me too, little man, me too." Patting Noah's back, Kip added, "But, we can pray. That's always a good solution because God can do more than we ever can!"

When Noah didn't speak, Kip asked him, "Do you remember the verses you've been working on this month for your Sunday school class? Jeremiah 29:12-13?"

Scrunching his face in concentration, Noah said, "Umm... Then you will call on me and come and... and..."

Kip chuckled and reminded him, "And pray to me..."

"Oh yeaaah." Closing his eyes, Noah continued, "Then you will call on me and come and pray to me, and I will listen to you. You will seek me and find me when you seek me with all your heart."

"Perfect, now what does it mean?"

Noah thought for a moment. "I guess it means that if I pray to God, He will listen to me, but I have to pray with my whole heart, that whole believing thing... faith."

"Exactly," Kip was proud of his growing son.

Noah nodded and whispered, "God, can you help my Grandpa? I miss him and his stories. I don't want him to be sad anymore. Amen."

Kip echoed the prayer in his own heart. "It's time for you to go to bed. You're going shoe shopping tomorrow."

Noah groaned.

Kip laughed but carried his son upstairs. Tucking him in for the night, he pulled the spaceship covers up to Noah's chin. "Sleep tight, little spaceman. I love you to the moon and back."

"Night, Dad. I love you to Neptune and back."

"I love you to Pluto and back."

As Noah snuggled deep down in the covers, he thought about what his dad said about God and prayer. *God does answer prayers, but sometimes it doesn't hurt to have a little help here on earth. I think it's time to call in Grandma Mags. Grandpa says God wants us to do what we can to help.*

Chapter Thirteen

"Tell me again why we're driving to the Atlanta airport on a Wednesday night?"

Becka cut her eyes at her husband and for the fourth time that day explained. "YOUR mother called on Sunday evening to say she, Rick, and April are coming to visit us for our winter break. We're picking them up at the airport tonight to spend the weekend with the family."

Kip looked in the rearview mirror before moving slowly into the exit lane for the airport. "Couldn't they have picked a better time to come. Traffic's horrendous."

"She's your mother."

"Now, Becka..."

"Don't get me wrong, I love your mother and family. It just seems this visit is way out of the blue and that's not like Mags. I wasn't expecting to see them until spring break at the earliest and that's two months away. Up north, we never got a winter break, it's just a Southern thing, apparently."

"Are you two fighting?" A quiet voice asked from the backseat.

Becka turned around to smile at Noah and Eva in the back of their midsize SUV. "No, sweetie. You know your father's a bit forgetful because he's so smart about other stuff. I'm thinking he had a conversation months ago about your Grandma coming for a visit and he doesn't want to admit he forgot to tell me anything about it."

"Becka, honey. I'm telling you I didn't forget..." Kip winked at Noah in the rearview mirror. "This time anyway. I promise, on Sunday when she called was the first I knew about this trip."

"Uh, huh."

"You'll see. She'll tell you when she gets here. Then I'll be vindicated."

"Well see, dear."

"Noah, my son, when you get married, make sure you marry a woman who isn't always right."

"Eww gross, Dad. I'm NOT getting married. I'm going to be an astronaut and explore Neptune."

As Becka and Kip chuckled, the conversation was halted with the approach to the airport. Parking in the short-term parking lot, the family got out and went to the welcome area for passenger arrivals. He moved them to the front so Eva and Noah could see when their grandparents arrived.

It will be good to see Mom. I'm not sure why she's visiting so abruptly like this, she's usually very organized and makes plans months in advance. When I told Dad, he just grunted and said he loved to see April. I'm a blessed man to have my divorced parents get along so well. Rick's like a second father and he and Dad have become good friends which is something highly unusual.

Before Kip could ponder his mother's actions any longer, he saw her riding up the escalator with Rick and April in tow. Noah and Eva started jumping up and down in anticipation. Maggie spread her arms wide as the two grandkids ran headlong into her arms. She bestowed hugs and kisses while Rick came to hug Kip, and April hugged Becka. The tall grandmother looked more like an Amazon than a grandmother. Her long hair had very little gray, and her figure looked fit and trim in a long sweater and leggings encased in brown boots, emphasizing long legs.

"We're so glad you made it. How was your flight?" Becka stepped back after hugging Rick.

"Good, a little bumpy, but it's nice to be in Georgia and not cold, windy Chicago." Rick smiled while putting his arm around April, he continued, "We were looking for an excuse to head south when Mags came up with this idea to visit you out of the blue."

Kip shot an "I told you so" look at Becka, before taking Noah's hand. "Well, let's get home. Have you guys eaten? We can stop for dinner once we get out of the heavy traffic."

Maggie nodded, still holding baby Eva. "That would be nice. The food on the plane was only a snack since it was such a short flight."

The family started walking to the car and Becka pondered the information about Maggie planning this trip on the spur of the moment. *Something's up, Lord. My mother senses are tingling.*

The family made it to Marietta before the kids needed to eat. Stopping at a family friendly restaurant, they enjoyed a good meal while catching up with each other. It hadn't been that long since the Miller family had flown down for a few days around Christmas. Laughter was plentiful, but Maggie could tell Becka was wondering about why they had made the sudden trip when she knew Chicago didn't get a winter break.

Which is why it wasn't surprising when Becka started fishing for information. "How were you able to get away from school, Rick? Chicago doesn't do winter breaks and a high school principal doesn't get to play hooky too often."

Rick cleared his throat, casting his eyes at his wife. "With April graduating college this summer, we decided to have a quick vacation before she started prepping for finals. She told us she wouldn't be able to do much for spring break this year with three final projects due. I made a few calls and here we are!"

Maggie changed the subject. "What are your plans this weekend, Son? We don't want to interrupt the family's plans with our impromptu visit."

"Yes, Kip." Rick looked relieved, "I don't want to mess up what you guys were going to do for the holiday break. We'll tag along when we can and be happy at your home when we can't."

Becka piped up, "No, you're fine. Kip works Thursday, but then has a few days off. I'll need to keep the kids entertained on Thursday, but Friday is a big movie night for kids at the church."

"Yes, Mrs. Andrea and Bailey are catering," Noah said with a mouthful of potatoes.

"Son, don't speak with your mouth full of food."

"Yes, Dad."

Maggie handed Noah a napkin. *Andrea, that's the woman Mark is taken with, according to my grandson. I wonder if I can crash this movie night at church and see the woman who has finally caught my ex-husband's eye? Lord, please work out a plan to help Mark, because he deserves to find love, too.*

"Shoot." Rising, Becka muttered, "I left Eva's blanket in the car and she's going to want it soon since she's almost finished eating." She handed Eva to Rick with a cry, "I'll be right back."

Maggie jumped up. "Let me help you."

The two ladies walked to the SUV and climbed in to find the missing blanket. "Found it," Maggie called out after a few moments before turning to Becka without warning. "I know you're wondering about the surprise visit."

Becka nodded in the darkened interior. "Yes, you've always been the planner."

"Noah called me Saturday afternoon."

"Oh?" *Thank You, Lord, she's always been blunt and to the point. I would've gone crazy wondering all week what was up.*

"Yes, he said Mark isn't acting like himself. He's not laughing or telling stories, or being the adoring Grandpa, he normally is, and Noah's worried."

"He's not drinking, I can promise you that."

"I know. I'm not worried about that. I know with God's help, he conquered that problem years ago."

"Then..."

"Noah said it was a woman. An Andrea Cabot?"

Becka leaned back in the passenger seat and sighed. "Yes, I think he's fallen for her but won't let himself admit it."

"I thought as much." Maggie began folding the blanket. "He's never dated or even looked at another woman since we divorced from what I know. I've never really understood why, though."

"You'd be okay..."

"Of course, I've been happily married to Rick for years now. We'll be celebrating our twenty-fifth anniversary next year. Mark deserves someone who can make him happy and according to Noah, Andrea Cabot is the woman to do it."

"If anyone could, it would be Andrea."

Maggie laughed, "That's what Noah thinks, too."

"So, my son has been playing matchmaker?"

"Looks like it."

"That explains a lot." *A whole lot!*

"I had a feeling you didn't know."

"So, what IS the plan, Mags? You always have one."

Maggie laughed, "Well, first I want to meet this Andrea woman. I have to admit I'm really curious."

"Well, Friday a big movie night for all the kids at church. Andrea and Bailey are providing the food, and Kip's helping chaperone."

With a twinkle in her brown eyes, Maggie asked, "Do they need any other volunteers?"

"I think something can be arranged."

"Good. I think it will help to see them together. Will Mark be there to help chaperone, as well?"

"Yes, but you should know they've been ignoring each other since New Year's and I'm not sure why. Before that, they were thick as thieves. I think they saw each other almost every day."

"Just as friends?"

Becka gave a loud belly laugh. "That's what they keep telling everyone, but I don't think anyone believes them."

The two ladies spoke a moment more about how best to have Maggie help chaperone before going back inside the restaurant to join their families. Maggie asked a lot of questions because she was determined to be well-prepared for her first encounter with the woman who finally turned Mark Hasting's head.

She had been worried when Noah called her last Saturday in tears talking about his upset Grandpa. Once she realized Mark wasn't hurt, she was able to piece the story together and figure out why exactly Noah was crying. She agreed with the little boy Mark wasn't acting like himself, but was surprised the eight-year-old knew it had to do with a woman.

"Grandma Mags, no one here knows what to do to fix this and I remember Grandpa told me once you know how to fix just about anything with the help of God, and I think it's going to take both of you."

She chuckled to herself for days after Noah made that remark already making plans to have the family go to Cartersville for a visit. *Thankfully, Rick takes my bossy ways in stride and only said he would enjoy some warmer weather. Mark would be embarrassed to know his grandson knew his problem before he did and I needed to get down here and see for myself what is going on. I can tell Becka's worried too, but she doesn't understand Mark as well as I do. If anyone's going to get the couple back on track, it will have to be me and the Lord, just like Noah thinks.*

When Maggie helped tuck Noah in for bed later that night, she wasn't surprised when his nightly prayers involved his grandpa getting back to normal.

Chapter Fourteen

"Andrea, sorry to call so early but I wanted to let Bailey know there will be a few extra people helping chaperone at the kid's movie tonight."

"Oh, that's good news, Becka. We had a family of volunteers back out because of illness."

"Perfect! That will put Maggie's mind at ease. She felt bad she and Rick would be crashing the event, but they wanted to spend as much time as they could with us for winter break."

"Maggie? Kip's mother, Maggie?"

"Yes, they surprised us with a quick visit. Rick says even our coldest winter weather is nothing like a Chicago winter."

Andrea agreed but wasn't listening attentively. *Maggie, Mark's ex-wife Maggie. Oh, Lord*!

Telling herself it didn't matter, Andrea said the extra help would be welcomed and quickly hung up the phone.

"I guess I need to let Bales know about the family canceling and the new volunteers willing to help," Andrea explained to Muffin who was busy chewing on one of her toys. Rising to her feet, she chuckled when Muffin rose with a wag of her tail. "Let's go find, Bales."

Muffin ran to the entrance to the big house, and once Andrea opened the door, she raced off to find Bailey. Heading to the kitchen, Andrea found her prepping for the movie event. "Bales, I just got off the phone with Becka Hastings. She's got family in town who can help chaperone tonight since one of the families backed out."

"That's good." Bailey turned to her husband. "Josh, can you get out the butter? I want to get the cookies done so all we'll have to do this evening is pop the popcorn."

Josh went to the commercial sized fridge but kept an eye on his mother. *She's been too quiet for a while now. She looks a little lost and I'm not sure why. I have noticed Mark hasn't been around lately and he was a fixture for a time. Did Mom and the boyfriend she isn't dating, break up?*

Andrea said, "I'm almost done with the goodie bags. Let me finish those and then I can help with the cookies."

Bailey nodded but didn't reply as Andrea was already walking to the living room. She waited until she knew Andrea was out of earshot before turning to Josh. "Something's wrong with Mom."

"I was just thinking that myself."

"Have you seen Mark around lately, besides at church?"

"No, but she still maintains they're just friends."

Josh looked up from mixing the dry ingredients for the cookies. "I'm not sure if they're even that anymore. I haven't seen them talk to each other in weeks."

Bailey froze trying to remember when she'd last seen them together. "I don't think they've seen each other since New Year's Eve."

Josh just grunted.

"Should we do something?"

"Oh, no, B." Josh lifted his hands in mock surrender, "I'm not messing in my mother's life again. I've learned my lesson."

Bailey winked, "Well that time you were wrong because I'm a lovely addition to your mother's life."

Josh came over to hug his new wife kissing her. "You were a lovely addition to my life as well."

"You better believe it."

"I think we just need to let Mom be and pray God works everything out. I don't want to see her hurt."

Bailey nodded fiercely, "No, I don't want that either. I just want her to be happy, not lonely."

"Me, too!"

Josh kissed her one last time. "We better get to making these cookies. There will be a lot of kids tonight."

"Muffin, NO!" Bailey cried out when she turned to see Muffin had gotten onto the chair in front of the breakfast bar to snag Josh's peanut butter sandwich. "Muffin, get down! DROP THAT SANDWICH!"

Josh started laughing and when Andrea came flying into the kitchen. She spied her sweet, little mutt chomping happily on what was left of Josh's sandwich.

She snorted, "The lady at the animal shelter said Muffin had a fondness for peanut butter." As the Muffin swallowed the last bite, Andrea pointed her finger. "I guess they weren't exaggerating when they said to worry about any open peanut butter jars."

Bailey looked aghast, unable to move, she kept opening her mouth but no sound came out. Josh moved back over to put his arm around his wife, trying to stop laughing. Finally, Bailey muttered, "I've never worried about food around her because she's always so well behaved. She just lays on the special pillow you bought her in the corner while we work."

Andrea gave her innocent looking dog a stern stare. "I should've known something was up when she didn't follow me into the living room to finish the bags. She follows me everywhere in the house when I'm home."

Sighing, Bailey almost forgave the dog for climbing on her clean counters when she saw Andrea laughing for the first time in weeks. She said a quick prayer for her friend and moved back to mixing the cookie dough. *I'll keep an eye on Mom tonight, and from now on, when there's peanut butter out, I'll be keeping an eye on Muffin!*

"Andrea, can you bring in the last of the bags. I need to set out some snacks for the early arrivals."

"Sure thing," Andrea replied to Bailey who was already moving to get the food table set up. They were at the church in plenty of time, but some parents were very excited to drop off their kids for an evening away. After two days of them cooped up at home, some parents had dropped them off extra early. Running out to the catering van parked near the fellowship hall side door, Andrea didn't see anyone behind her until she heard a regal voice ask, "Can we help?"

Andrea turned and saw one of the most stunning women she had ever seen. Tall, dark blonde hair, the woman had alabaster skin that looked like it had never seen the sun and was in a winter outfit straight out of an expensive catalog. "Thank you. I do have quite a few gift bags to carry in and this will save me several trips."

"Great." She turned to call behind her, "Okay gang, grab a box. Rick make sure April helps, too!"

Oh Lord, this must be Maggie! Andrea stood back as the tall amazon directed Rick and her daughter, April, to help. All Andrea could say was a quick, "Thank you."

"You're welcome! You must be, Andrea. I know who you are because of Noah. He's quite fond of you."

"Oh, yes. He's a sweet boy." Andrea looked around, "Is he here?"

"Yes, Mark's getting him out of his coat. He's so excited to see you and Brian it's taking a herculean effort by his grandpa to get him settled."

Andrea laughed softly, "I remember those days."

She didn't say anything more but followed the group inside while she made a promise to herself to avoid the woman who made her feel small and not worthy of Mark Hastings at all. *No wonder he went running. It's a good thing we aren't meant to be anything, not even friends, anymore. A famous author should be dating a stunning Amazon, not a short caterer.* She frowned but reminded herself, *you don't want to date anyone anyway, you like your life, remember?!?*

Moving to set out the goodie bags, Andrea sighed, *it's going to be a long night.*

Mark put a tuckered-out Noah to bed before making his way downstairs. He was surprised to see the living room was now empty except for his ex-wife sitting on the sofa drinking some hot chocolate Becka had made when they got home from the children's movie night.

"What's up, Mags? You've been quiet this evening and now the rest of the family disappears in the few moments I was tucking in Noah."

"Did you tell him a funny story tonight?"

Mark frowned, "No, but he was practically asleep before his head hit the pillow after tonight's fun."

She tucked her feet under her. "When was the last time you put him to bed with a funny, made-up-on-the-fly story?"

Feeling a bit defensive, Mark didn't answer right away. *It's been weeks. Not since New Year's.*

"That's what I thought."

"What does that mean? I didn't even say anything."

"I met Andrea tonight."

"Oh?" *Lord, I don't think I've had a more confusing conversation in my life.*

"Yes, and she's lovely, sweet, kind, funny, and do I need to go on?"

Sighing, Mark sat down across from Maggie. "Where's this going, Mags?"

"Why haven't you asked her out?"

"What?"

"You heard me, Mark Lawson Hastings."

"I'm pretending I didn't."

"We've always been honest with each other since the divorce. You're a good friend, not just the father of my son. Talk to me."

"I don't know what to say."

"Yes, you do, Mr. Author. You always know what to say."

"That's just the thing. I have NO words. I haven't written a single sentence of my new book series since December." Covering his face, he muttered, "I had all of these great ideas, but they seemed to have disappeared."

"When you stopped seeing Andrea?"

"We're just friends, but we're not even that anymore. She has nothing to do with my writer's block though," Mark defended himself before dropping onto the couch.

"I think they're related."

"I don't."

"I've never asked, but I've always wondered why you never dated. After all this time, I've never known you to go out on even ONE date with a woman!"

"Well, if I can't have you…"

"Please, we both know that's not true. We aren't meant to be anything more than friends."

Mark leaned back on the couch and sighed, "Yes, we are better friends than we were husband and wife."

"But that doesn't mean you couldn't have found someone…"

"Oh, yes, it does. Look at me, Mags. I'm an alcoholic and I don't deserve to find happiness in marriage. I had my chance." He looked down at his hands. "I've got my writing, Kip, his family, and your family. I'm fine."

"A writer that's not writing, isn't fine."

"I'm just in a slump."

"What's the verse you learned shortly after you were saved?"

"The one from Titus?" *Where's she going now? I feel like I'm on a roller coaster with this conversation.*

"Yes, say it."

Frowning, Mark closed his eyes, quoting from memory, "Not by works of righteousness which we have done but according to His mercy He saved us, by the washing of regeneration, and renewing of the Holy Ghost."

"Do you know it was that verse which let me know you had really changed and convinced me to let you have the belated Christmas with Kip that first year."

Mark's head whipped up to look at Maggie. He noticed tears in her warm, brown eyes, but didn't speak as she continued, "I saw the sheets of paper all over your apartment when I came over to pick up the monthly child support check for Kip. At first, I thought it was for a new story, but I saw where you had written the verse out, over and over again. There were hundreds of pages of that verse."

"It spoke to me. It's what brought me to my knees when I hit rock bottom. My sponsor through AA was a Christian and had me attend church with him to keep me from drinking on Sunday mornings when it was still hard for me to stay away from the bottle. The pastor quoted Titus 3:5 and it was like God spoke from Heaven and said, 'You can't clean yourself up on your own, but let ME help you because I love you and want to make you new again.'" Tears in his eyes, Mark said quietly, "In AA they talk about taking it one day at a time, and the word renewal means over and over, again and again. I knew as an alcoholic I would need God's help every single day for the rest of my life."

Maggie stood up and came over to sit beside Mark, "We ALL need God to renew us every day, no matter what's in our past and we ALL have one. Being an alcoholic is not who you are in God, you're His child, the son of a King."

"But, Mags, I really messed up. I remember how angry and violent I was. It was why you left me and took Kip."

"Yes, but that was more than twenty years ago. You're not the same man, BECAUSE you let God renew your life, daily. When you became saved, God wiped it away. You're not to live with those shackles anymore. He broke those off you."

"But Andrea doesn't know about my past."

"From what little I know of Andrea, she won't hold it against you. You're not the man I married. You're a better one by the renewing grace of God."

Mark didn't speak and Maggie gently added, "Stop letting the devil win the battle when God's already won the war."

"You're a good woman, Mags. I don't deserve your friendship after everything that's happened."

"Please." She waved her hand at him, "I've been blessed to have you in my life. Rick thinks of you as a good friend and April calls you, Uncle Mark. She loves telling people about her famous uncle."

"I don't think Andrea's interested in me as anything more than friends."

"Oh? What makes you think that?"

"I kissed her and she ran."

"What?" Sitting back to look at him, Maggie asked, "When did this happen?"

"New Year's Eve, a party at her home."

"And this is when you started having writer's block?"

Mark blushed, "Yes, but it's not..."

"Not related, I know." Maggie couldn't hide her chuckle. "I don't know exactly what Andrea thought of the kiss, but I know at the movie tonight, she spent most of the evening watching you when you weren't watching her."

Mark felt hope rising in his chest, "Really?"

Giggling, Maggie said, "Yes, Mark, really. Have you two talked since this kiss? Ever talked about dating at all?"

"No, I didn't think I should..."

"She'd be blessed to have you in her life."

"I feel the same way about her."

Lord, I've got my work cut out for me on this vacation. Maggie stood, "It's getting late. I'll be praying about it and your writer's block."

"Thanks, Mags."

She let Mark out of the house and locked up for the night. Climbing the stairs to her bed, she prayed for God to show her what to do.

Chapter Fifteen

"Wow, Lord. This is some place." Maggie parked Mark's jeep outside the front of Andrea's home and was stunned by the setup.

"She's got the big house, adorable barn, and it looks like they're building another large structure in the back."

Known for talking out loud to God, Maggie got out of the jeep and strode purposely up to the front door. Knocking, she prayed, "I leave tomorrow, Lord, help me to do what You brought me here to do before I leave."

After a few moments, the door opened and a petite redhead stood there with a mixing bowl in her hands. "Sorry, I'd shake your hand to welcome you in, but I've got to keep mixing this or I will lose the entire batch."

"It's okay."

"Are you here to see Andrea?" Bailey stepped back to let the tall, blonde inside the door. She paused, "You look familiar. Were you at the movie night on Friday evening?"

"Yes, I'm Maggie Miller."

"Oh, Noah's grandmother."

Maggie chuckled, "Yes, also known as the ex-wife."

Bailey blushed but secretly liked the direct woman. *Do I need to block the door to keep her from coming in?* Eyeing her discreetly, Bailey stepped back, "Come in. Does Andrea know you're coming?"

"No, this is an impromptu visit."

"Do I need to get the pitchfork?" Bailey eyed her appraisingly. *She had better not be here to upset Mom. I could take the Amazon if I had to.*

Maggie laughed out loud. "Good Lord, no. I'm here to tell your mother-in-law how wonderful Mark really is and see if I can't help the two of them patch up whatever went wrong in January."

"Well, in that case, come in. Mom's in her cottage doing some paperwork, but I'm sure she'd love the distraction."

We'll see. Maggie kept the comment to herself but followed the spunky redhead through the front of the house to a small hallway off the side.

"This is the entrance to the mother-in-law suite, but we just call it the cottage. Andrea has never been a mother-in-law to me." Knocking, Bailey turned to Maggie, blocking the door. "She means a lot to me."

"Understood." *She couldn't be clearer if she tried. I wonder if Andrea knows how fiercely she's loved.*

"It's open."

Bailey poked her head into Andrea's living room. "Hey, Mom. You have a visitor. I'm going to leave the door open. Yell if you need me."

Puzzled by Bailey's comment, Andrea didn't understand until Maggie stepped into her living room. *Shoot, Lord, why did I still have to be in yoga pants from my walk with Muffin this morning? I wish I owned a pair of four-inch heels to wear around this Amazon.*

Andrea stood and motioned for the woman to sit down. "Would you like something to drink? Tea, coffee..."

"Coffee would be nice."

Walking to the small kitchen, Andrea pulled out an extra mug and started the second pot of the morning. She watched as Maggie sat on the sofa and began to pet Muffin. *What's going on here?*

"You have a sweet dog."

"Thank you, she's from the animal shelter. I've only had her a few months."

"What's her name?"

"Muffin."

"That's cute for a caterer."

Andrea smiled at the elegant woman talking sweetly to her pup. *She can't be that bad if Muffin likes her. But, Lord, why is she here to see me? I avoided her like the plague at the movie event last night.*

Carrying the coffee and all of the fixings, Andrea sat the tray down and moved to sit on the other side of Muffin. She had just picked up the coffee mug to pass to Maggie when the woman spoke up.

"I'm here because it's come to my attention Mark hasn't been acting like himself lately."

"Oh?" Andrea stared at her coffee, intently watching the bubbles.

"Yes, Noah called me last week very upset."

Andrea's head snapped up, "Noah's upset?"

She cares for my grandson, that's a good sign. Taking a sip, Maggie paused, "The coffee's excellent by the way."

"Thank you, now what's wrong with Noah?" Andrea watched Maggie carefully, "I thought you said this was about Mark?"

Hiding a smile that Andrea could be fierce when it came to her grandson, Maggie explained, "Noah called to say his grandpa hadn't been himself since New Year's and he's worried. It seems Mark hasn't been able to write a word of his new story and that isn't like the Mark, I know."

Hiding a blush, Andrea looked away, "Well, I hear writer's block is a real thing." *Poor Noah, he must be worried his grandpa won't be able to finish the novel that features him.*

"Not for Mark it isn't. I've never seen anyone meant to be a writer more than him. That man was put on this earth to create stories."

Andrea didn't speak, and Maggie started petting Muffin with one hand. "To be perfectly honest, I believe he's not able to write because of you."

"Me?" Andrea squeaked.

"It seems he's quite taken with you."

Blushing to her roots, Andrea stood and walked to the kitchen. "I don't think so."

Amused, Maggie leaned back, crossing her legs. "Why not?"

Frustrated, she turned to face Mark's ex-wife and exclaimed, "Well, for one thing, he kissed me on New Year's Eve and then the man ran away."

She cares for him, too! She just doesn't want to admit it. With a twinkle in her eye Maggie said, "Mark told me about the kiss and how he hasn't been the same since."

"He hasn't?" Hope was clearly heard in Andrea's softly spoken words.

Putting down her coffee mug, Maggie turned to face Andrea standing in the kitchen. In a clear, firm voice she said, "Mark's miserable because he thinks he's too messed up to ask you out."

"Messed up? Why? He's kind, loving, funny, witty…" Andrea stopped, blushing again to her roots. *Lord, why is it talking about the man makes me blush like a silly teenager?!?*

"I know Mark never told you he's an alcoholic and has been attending…"

"AA, I know that."

It was Maggie's turn to be shocked, "How did you know? Mark never said anything, but did Kip or Becka say something to you?"

Shaking her head, Andrea said, "He uses all the phrases. Let go and let God, progress not perfection, one day at a time, keep it simple, and do the next right thing…"

Seeing Maggie's mouth hanging open, Andrea laughed softly, "I was a military wife and have seen my share of AA members. One of my husband's good friends was long-term member as well as one of my uncles."

Maggie nodded. "And it doesn't bother you?"

"No, it seems to be something he's gotten help for."

"Then why are the two of you dancing around this? It's obvious you care for each other."

Unsure about this direct woman, Andrea moved to sit in the small armchair as she thought for a moment. *Why am I dancing around this, Lord? I know I like my independence and making my own decisions. I've already had one husband who could be a bit overbearing and demanding, and I don't want another one.*

"You do care for him, don't you Andrea?" Maggie watched the emotions on the woman's face and started to wonder if she and the others were all wrong about the couple's mutual feelings for each other.

"Yes," Andrea whispered, closing her eyes. "Yes, but I'm not looking to date. I like my independence and not having to run every decision past a husband before I do something. I loved James and miss him, but he could be demanding and overprotective at times."

"That isn't Mark. He's one of the kindest, easiest going guys I know."

"I have seen that," Andrea whispered.

"I'll be the first to admit when he was drinking, he was mean and violent. I divorced him and took Kip away to protect us both. He wasn't that way when I married him, it was only when Kip was about five and Mark's mother died from a sudden heart attack, things changed."

Moving closer to Andrea, Maggie continued, "He admitted to me years later he was angry at God for taking away his only loving parent, and he couldn't deal with the anger he still had directed at both his earthly father and his Heavenly one. Anger and feeling helpless sent him to a very dark place."

With tears in her eyes, Maggie said quietly, "I prayed for my ex-husband to be saved, but it was a few years later after I had remarried, he hit rock bottom, and joined AA, which led him to turn his life around."

She looked Andrea in the eye, "I truly believe in God's power, because Mark's life is the perfect example of God's renewing grace, every single day. I've watched him grow in the Lord and learn to conquer his alcoholism with the grace of God and I'm honored to call him a friend. He is one of the strongest, most down to earth, real Christian men I know."

"I know he's a good man..." Andrea decided to be honest, "But, I'm set in my ways and can be stubborn. I worked hard to set up this catering business, it's my dream...

"Mark won't hold you back from your dreams, if anything, he'd help you achieve them."

Andrea didn't speak, but Maggie could see tears in her eyes. "Mark was my biggest cheerleader when it came to my family. He's an uncle to my daughter, and when she was going through a very rebellious stage, he was the encouragement Rick and I needed to get through a dark time together."

Seeing the woman had a lot to think about, Maggie stood up. "I wanted to stop by and tell you what a good man Mark is. My family and I are leaving tomorrow, but

I wanted you to know I'd love to consider you a friend, no matter how things end up with Mark. You've been good for Noah, and while you might not realize it yet, I believe you're good for Mark, too."

Andrea stood up, "I'd like to be friends, Maggie." *I've misjudged her, Lord. She's as kind-hearted as she is stunning. I'd be blessed to have her as a friend.*

"My friends call me, Mags."

"I feel I owe you an apology, Mags."

"Not at all." Maggie extended her hand, "I can be a bit forward, my husband reminds me to slow down, but I have a hard time listening."

"Maybe, but I wasn't the most welcoming."

"You were protecting your heart and I get that, I just want you to know that Mark's worth taking a leap of faith."

"Thanks, Mags."

Seeing the radiant smile on Andrea's face, Maggie could see why Mark fell for the woman. *She's beautiful on the inside and out.* "We'll be at church tomorrow before Kip and Becka drive us to the airport."

"I'll look forward to saying hello before you leave."

"I'd like that, Andrea. I really would." Picking up her purse, Maggie paused, "Mark really is a good man, and I think you both would be blessed to have each other. I just ask you think and pray about what I've said."

"I can do that, Mags. Most definitely, I can do that."

Hugging the petite woman, Maggie gathered her things and left out the cottage front door. As she got into the jeep to leave, she glanced at the blue sky, "Lord, I did as You asked, spoke my peace. It's up to the three of you now and I pray You help guide those two stubborn people to their own happily ever after."

<u>Mark's Journal Entry - February 22, 2014</u>

Lord,

Mags and her family are leaving tomorrow and I'm grateful for the unexpected trip they made out here. It still amazes me the friendship I have with my ex-wife and Rick. Maggie allowing me to be a part of her family for all these years made my life a little less lonely.

I've been doing a lot of thinking about the conversation we had late Friday night. It's so easy to say You make all things new, but so much harder to live it out. I know once I ask forgiveness for my sins You forget them, and it's only me who keeps bringing them up over and over. I haven't had a drink in twenty-four years, one month, and eight days, but it seems I can't forgive myself even after You and my family have forgiven me. I never thought this would be the hardest lesson for me to learn.

I'll see Andrea at church tomorrow. Kip and Becka have started sitting with her and her family since the first day. I can't avoid her forever, and if I'm honest, I don't want to. I've missed her these past few weeks, her laugh, her smile, the quiet way she encourages me to be my best me. I realized today, even if I didn't write another word, I would still want Andrea in my life!

I was going to tell Mags, but she went somewhere this afternoon and I'm not sure where, just she took my jeep. I'll tell her before she leaves tomorrow. I know she'd be happy to know I've made this decision.

Please help me to stop living in the past and see if it's possible to move forward with Andrea in my life. I'd really like to try! As Mags reminded me, Your renewing power is never-ending and as long as I accept it every day, I can be a man worthy of Andrea.

Chapter Sixteen

"Mom, do you want to ride with us this morning?"

Andrea looked up from her breakfast in the catering kitchen to see Josh and Bailey staring at her intently. "Sorry, what?"

"B asked if you wanted to ride with us to church this morning?"

Pushing her eggs around the plate, Andrea said, "Yes, that would be nice."

"Are you okay, Mom? You've been awful quiet."

"Yes, I'm fine, Josh. Just thinking about things."

"Does it have to do with Maggie Miller being here yesterday?" Bailey asked putting up breakfast dishes.

Josh's head whipped around to look at his mother, "Mark's ex-wife was here yesterday! How am I always the last to know these things?"

Bailey laughed, "Josh, we talked about this last night as we were going to bed. This is proof you never listen to me after ten."

"I was tired."

"Children."

Josh and Bailey looked up, smiling sheepishly, "Sorry, Mom."

Andrea gave a wistful smile, "It's fine. And I'm fine. Just thinking about somethings Mags pointed out."

"Mags?"

"Yes, I think Maggie and I are going to be good friends. I like her."

"And her ex-husband?"

"JOSH!" Bailey and Andrea shouted at the same time.

Josh walked over to sit by his mother at the kitchen island. "Mom, I don't want to get into your business, I've truly learned my lesson."

Seeing her chuckle, Josh continued, "I want you to know, I think Mark's a great guy and it has nothing to do with him being my favorite author of all time. If he makes you happy, then know Bailey and I would be happy for you."

Hugging her, he whispered, "And I think Dad would be, too! He loved anything that made you smile."

Tears in her eyes, Andrea hugged her son, "Thank you, sweetheart. You've certainly become wise since you've gotten married."

Bailey laughed, "He had to, or else we would never have gotten back together."

Joining in the laughter, Andrea felt better for having the talk with Josh. *I've been wondering what he might think if I did start dating Mark. I've thought a lot about what Mags said yesterday and she's right, Mark and James are completely different. I might need to remember that.*

Walking back to her part of the house to grab her coat and Bible, she whispered a prayer, "Lord, I'm not sure what will happen with Mark and I. It's a scary thought to consider dating someone at my age, but well..."

Andrea stopped speaking and remembered Mark smiling at her the first time they met. She remembered looking into his blue eyes as they shook hands and feeling a strange peace mixed up in her nervousness. Before she could ponder that thought any further, Josh was yelling it was time to leave for church. Sending up a prayer for God's will, Andrea grabbed her Bible before jumping in the back of the car.

Later when Andrea was walking down to the sanctuary, she was surprised she hadn't seen Noah's family. Often Noah snuck into her classroom to say hello before he went to children's church. A little worried, she felt relieved when she saw Becka, Kip and the entire Miller family standing in the vestibule talking to Pastor Graham. *I wonder where Mark is?*

Walking up, Becka turned to hug her and whispered, "We were running late this morning. Mags, Rick, and April had to load all their luggage to leave from here to drive to the airport. Noah's spending the night with Brian so he won't be up late for school tomorrow. Mark was loading his overnight bag into Laura's car for her."

"It's good he gets to spend so much time with Brian. They're good for each other."

Becka nodded and whispered back, "Yes, the two boys are the best of friends and I can't tell you how relieved I am. As a children's counselor, I've been worried about how alone he is, but he seemed to just have been waiting for the perfect best friend."

Nodding hello to the pastor, Andrea followed everyone into the sanctuary to their normal pew behind Grace and Delia Anne. Hugging the two ladies, Andrea settled down on the end talking to Maggie and Rick about how they enjoyed their trip. As the music was starting for worship, she looked over and saw Mark standing next to her with a large smile on his face.

"May I sit with you?"

Andrea nodded and wasn't too surprised everyone had already moved down to make room for him to sit on the end next to her. His deep baritone voice was soothing and she enjoyed his singing during worship which only made it harder for her to focus during the sermon with him so near. *Lord, can this be resolved today? I can't keep acting like a teenager at my age.*

In Andrea's mind the service went too quickly, and before she knew it, everyone was standing for the closing prayer. The pastor had everyone grab hands across the aisles and as Andrea slid her petite hand into Mark's outstretched one, she felt comforted by his firm grip, feeling the same peace as from that first handshake months ago. Mark squeezed her hand and then released it. Before she had a chance to think about it, Maggie walked up with Rick and April behind her.

"It was wonderful to meet you, Andrea. You're a talented and lovely woman."

Andrea blushed. "Thank you, Mags. You've given me a lot to think about."

"That's what friends do."

The two ladies hugged before Andrea said goodbye to April and Rick. Kip was trying to get everyone to the car quickly to leave for the airport before traffic got too bad because of construction. She watched out of the corner of her eye as Mark said goodbye to Maggie's family. April grabbed him for a big hug, and Mark laughing told her she was growing too beautiful. Rick quickly agreed and the two men hugged before Mark turned to Maggie.

Unable to hear what the ex-couple said, Andrea told herself she wasn't jealous and turned to walk away after waving goodbye to Becka and Kip one last time. Before she made it out of the sanctuary, she heard someone call her name and turned to see Mark rushing down the aisle toward her. "Andrea, wait, please. I wanted to talk to you a moment."

Andrea stopped in full view of the Hasting-Miller family and tried to hide a blush from rising to her cheeks. *Shoot, Lord, does everyone have to see me acting like a teenager?!?*

Mark closed the distance between them. "I was wondering if you had plans for lunch?" He flashed a handsome smile her way. "I've been abandoned for lunch today and decided I want to take a lovely lady out for a meal."

"Oh," Andrea looked around. "I'm sure you can find someone..."

"Andrea, I want to take YOU out to eat. Can we talk? We've never talked about what happened at the New Year's Eve party and well, I have some things I need to tell you."

The wistful look in his eyes stopped any protest on her lips, and Andrea nodded yes.

"Is there somewhere you'd like to go?"

"What do you like? Seafood, Mexican, Chinese?"

"Good Chicago pizza."

Andrea laughed, "I don't believe we have one in Cartersville."

"I'll have to cook for you one night. I make a mean deep-dish pepperoni pizza."

"But that doesn't help us to eat right now."

"No, but there's a Chinese place near here that's good. Do you like Chinese?"

"I do."

"Do want to meet me over there or...?"

"Actually, Bailey and Josh drove me."

"I'd be delighted to drive you. I can even take you home after."

"Okay, let me tell Bales and Josh."

Andrea pulled out her phone to text the couple she had a ride and would see them later. She didn't add who she was spending time with for lunch. When Mark led her to the parking lot, Andrea was grateful it was almost empty.

The couple rode in awkward silence. Andrea found herself struggling with what to say. *We used to be good friends, Lord. Has that kiss ruined everything?*

After Mark pulled into the parking lot, he got out to help Andrea from the jeep. He steered her inside and Andrea sent up a prayer this meal wouldn't be a total disaster filled with either awkward silence or stilted conversation. Once seated, she unfolded her napkin for something to hold onto when Mark finally spoke.

"I've spent the car ride trying to get up the courage to tell you..." Mark paused, before admitting quietly, "I'm not very good at this."

Andrea looked at him, sympathy for the man welling up in her as she put her hand on his. "We're friends, Mark. Nothing has changed that. You can tell me anything you want."

Mark looked relieved and after the waitress took their drink order, he took Andrea's hand. "First, I want to tell you I'm sorry about how that first kiss went. I shouldn't have let it happen that way and I never meant to frighten you."

"I wasn't frightened, just a little shocked. I'd been telling everyone all night we were just friends and then that kiss happened." *He said the first kiss.* "And it wasn't a 'we're just friends' kind of kiss."

He bellowed, "Definitely not kissing a friend! I'd been telling myself we were just friends, because I didn't feel like I could ever date again, let alone re-marry."

"You mean because you're an alcoholic?"

Mark's mouth fell open, "Mags told you? I found out by accident she went to see you yesterday."

"Not really. I figured it out by all of our talks before Christmas. You say a lot of the phrases of an AA member."

When he continued to look dumbfounded, she explained, "I had an Uncle in AA and knew some other people who were in the program."

"So, if I told you I was interested in you as more than a friend, you wouldn't run away screaming?"

Andrea knew he was trying to be funny to hide his fear. "Mark, I think you're a wonderful man and have spent the entire time I've known you, telling myself not to act like a silly teenage girl with a crush on a celebrity!"

"Andrea, I'm no celebrity."

"Humph." She snorted. "Yes, you are, but you're also a funny, kind grandpa and father."

"Well, thank you. It took me a while to get there."

"But you got there through God's renewing grace."

A large smile brightened his face. "I should've known you would understand."

"Maggie did come to see me yesterday to tell me what a wonderful man you are. While I already knew about the recovering alcoholism, I had to do some real soul searching of my own to see if I wanted to start dating again."

"Because of James?"

"Yes, but not in the way you might think."

She sighed, "My marriage to James was a good one, but we had our ups and downs like any couple. He wasn't perfect and I guess after being widowed for a few years, I started to idolize him and forget some of his faults."

Right then the waitress came to get their orders, and they stopped talking long enough to decide on lunch. Andrea waited until it was just the two of them and then said quietly, "My husband wasn't the best father to Josh. He could also be controlling and overprotective. After a few years of not being a wife, I've grown to like my independence and doing what I want, when I want."

"I can understand that."

Andrea smiled at him, her brown eyes warm. "Mags said you would and I have to admit, I believe her."

"Does that mean you'd be willing to try this dating thing with me?"

Tucking a piece of curly brown hair behind her ear, Andrea said firmly, "Yes, I believe I'd like to try this new adventure with you."

Mark's grin was from ear to ear. "I think it would worth taking a chance on. I know God brought you into my life for a reason and I think I'm going to enjoy finding out why."

When the food arrived, the waitress noticed the smiles and laughter, but the new couple only had eyes for each other. The rest of the meal was more like their original talks before the kiss, but the kiss was never far from their minds.

"I have something with Noah at his school on Friday night, but was wondering if we could have our official first date Saturday evening?"

Andrea took the last sip of hot tea. "I'd like that."

Mark rose and helped Andrea into her coat. "I'll call you this week to set up plans."

Walking her to his car, Mark said a quick thank you prayer for Mags and Noah. The drive to drop Andrea off, and then home, went quickly as he thought of plans for their first date. *I'm going to be counting the hours, Lord, I can tell.*

Chapter Seventeen

"I'm so glad you made it!" Mark cried out opening the door.

"It was sweet of you to change plans so I could bring Muffin," Andrea put her beagle down on the floor. "Aiden and Carrie brought the twins over to visit with Bailey and Josh. Muffin's good with kids, but the twins are in a grabbing and tugging phase. I didn't want them to lock her up in the cottage where she'd be able to hear all the fun she was missing out on."

Mark squatted down to pet the dog. Muffin turned her head to allow him to scratch behind her ears, her favorite spot.

"You're a kind woman, Andrea. It was easy to change plans. I just canceled our dinner reservations and grabbed some groceries."

Andrea arched an eyebrow, "You cook?"

Laughing, Mark stood up, "I've been a bachelor for over twenty years so I had to learn or I would've starved. I can make the basics and when I get tired of my own cooking, I either eat out or with Kip's family. Becka's a sweetheart and takes pity on me at least once or twice a week."

Andrea gave Muffin her favorite chew toy. "Is there something I can do to help with dinner?"

Mark led her through the entryway to the living room. "The kitchen's tiny for two cooks, but there's a breakfast bar where you can sit and keep me company."

"I can do that!" Putting her purse down, she called, "Come on, Muffin."

"She'll be fine. There's really nothing she can get into."

"Thankfully, she's a good dog and I don't worry about anything but Kleenex. She loves to shred them when she can find some."

As Mark washed his hands, Andrea hopped up on the stool. "The first time I left her alone, I came back and it looked like it had snowed all over the inside of the cottage."

"Neptune was based on a dog I had growing up. He loved Kleenex, too, but we couldn't figure out where he was getting them from."

Mark went to the fridge and when he came back with an armload of supplies, he continued, "One day, I must have surprised him, because he didn't know I'd walked into the room and he went to his Kleenex stash behind our couch!"

Andrea was laughing so hard, there were tears in her eyes, "What a smart dog."

"That's what I thought, and it led to Neptune, the talking dog."

Uncovering a bowl, Mark pulled out some dough he made earlier and was letting rise. "I thought I'd make my best meal for you – deep, dish Chicago pizza!"

"I don't think I've ever had Chicago style pizza before."

"I can't believe it." Mark's jaw fell open, "We'll have to fix this serious problem tonight and then you'll never go back. I can't have my girlfriend not understand the amazing perfection that is Chicago style pizza."

Blushing, she was pleased by his comment. "We'll see. I do have a sophisticated palate being around Bailey."

Mark stopped kneading the dough to smirk, "I saw her chowing down on a cheeseburger the other day!"

Snorting, Andrea replied, "But that's an essential food group!"

They spent the next thirty minutes talking about favorite foods while Mark put together the pizza. When he pulled out salad fixings, Andrea started chopping veggies at her seat. Muffin sat at Andrea's feet, watching the floor intently for dropped food. Disappointed Mark wasn't messier in the tiny kitchen, she drifted off to sleep.

"What brought you from Chicago?" Andrea asked.

"Becka finished her counseling degree and got a good job down here. Kip being an orthopedic surgeon can find work anywhere. They liked the look of Cartersville and decided to move for their family to have a big yard and good schools." Mark whipped up a quick salad dressing, "I was in a transitional point in my life and thought I'd follow, that way Kip and Becka wouldn't need to have a daycare take care of the kids all the time."

"I know Noah and Eva adore seeing their Grandpa most every day."

"I'm the blessed one." Mark looked up at Andrea with a grin. "Kids grow too fast to only see them at holidays. I missed so much of Kip's life and don't want to miss out on seeing Noah and Eva grow up."

"Yes, my boys grew up on me too fast."

"Being an army brat and then army wife, what's been the favorite place for you to live?"

"Ohh, that's hard. I enjoyed the traveling when I was a kid, I made friends easily and enjoyed time to myself. I loved exploring new places. It was harder once I had the boys and had to uproot them every few years."

"Were you ever stationed outside of the US?"

Andrea nodded, "Yes, in Turkey and Guam with my dad for a bit. I loved Turkey, but Guam had too many lizards for my liking. People who lived there didn't think much of finding them in the house, but I thought they were gross and didn't mind we only stayed about eight months."

Finished with the salad prep, Andrea took the bowl Mark had set out and starting combining all the vegetables. "How's the NOAH book going?"

Mark grabbed plates and moved to set the little dinette table for two in the corner of the kitchen. "Not as well as I would like. I'm supposed to have the entire first draft done by the end of March which gives me a month to finish. I'm not even halfway done, but I've prayed about it. I know my editor understands this is unusual for me and would give me an extension if I asked, I've just never needed to ask before."

Andrea turned at the counter to face him, "It must be hard struggling with something that has always come so easily before."

Mark sat at the little table. "Yeah. Once I was saved, I wrote my next novel in a week. It was incredible. I've never done that before or since, but I've also never had to struggle with writing like this. I'd get stuck, but would just take a day or two to focus on something else and the words would come."

"Maybe God is trying to teach you a new lesson?"

He laughed, "I hope not, because I think I'm failing the test." The oven beeped and he grabbed oven mittens. "Dinner's ready. Are you hungry?"

"Yes, and it smells wonderful."

"Just wait until you try it."

Mark stood to grab the pizza and Andrea brought the salad over. Putting some on their plates, she placed the large bowl back on the counter and sat while Mark brought the pizza. He sat down across from her. "Ready to pray?"

After Andrea's nod, Mark took her hand and bowed his head. "Lord, thank You for this food and the kind woman I'm sharing it with. Thank You for bringing me to Cartersville to meet this special lady. May our relationship always be centered around You. Bless this food and us to Your service. Amen."

Touched by his prayer, Andrea said amen and then took a bite of hot pizza. Slightly burning her tongue, she said, "It's good. I'm glad you like everything on your pizza. I do too, but Josh and Bailey can be picky."

"I don't like pineapple but other than that, I'm game for most anything on a pizza!"

"Me either, I think pineapple should only go in desserts."

"What about Jacob? Was he a picky eater?"

She ate some of her salad. "No. He ate just about anything and everything. He was constantly on the move while saying he was hungry."

"Kip was like that. I couldn't get the boy to the table fast enough when he was STAAAAARVING as he would tell me."

"Yes, it amazes me how kids can hold out a word for so long."

"Jacob's in the military like his dad?"

"Yes, Marines. Like father, like son. I haven't heard from him in a while. He sent a quick email a few months ago he was going on a long mission and it would be a while before I'd hear from him."

"That must be hard. I struggled not seeing my son for a time, but I at least knew where he was and he was safe."

Andrea nodded, a few tears falling down her cheeks. Mark jumped up to grab a tissue and gently wiped away a few tears. Andrea smiled a watery thanks. "Sorry, it's just been hard lately. He's been out of touch like this before, but I don't think he knows Josh got married and we weren't able to invite him to the wedding."

Mark took her hand, "I'll be praying he's able to make contact soon. Even if it's only to say, 'hi mom, I'm fine'."

"Thank you." She whispered.

"It's hard not seeing your son, no matter what age he is."

Andrea had a slight smile as she said, "That's true. Poor Bailey, when she first arrived, she thought my boys were teenagers because I still talk about them like they're kids. It led to a lot of confusion."

Mark taking a bite of the salad grunted, "I can't imagine."

"It was a mess because when they finally met, Bailey accidentally knocked hot pasta all over his suit and ruined a pair of his dress shoes." Laughing with Mark, she continued, "It still amazes me they ended up married."

As Andrea took a bite of pizza, Mark said, "That's a great story, I might steal it for one of my own books one day."

"Josh would love that, even if it is about him getting clobbered."

They discussed more about their kids growing up, telling funny stories about Kip, Josh, and Jacob. The dinner passed too quickly in their minds and before they knew it, it was time to clean up the dishes. Andrea insisted on helping since Mark cooked.

"I can't believe Muffin isn't sitting by the dishwasher. She loves it when Josh puts away the dishes because he lets her lick the plates if Bailey isn't around."

As Mark was drying his hands, Andrea called out, "Muffin, here girl, where are you?"

When the little dog didn't come running, Andrea began to worry. "I hope she hasn't gotten into trouble. She never gets into anything at home, but..."

"Don't worry, Andrea. There's nothing for her to get into. Remember, I have young grandkids."

Taking her hand, Mark led her out of the kitchen. "Let's go look for her. She can't be in too many places, this is a small house."

Cutting back through the living room, the couple looked in the guest bathroom, and Mark's bedroom, before walking into the back room that contained his office. Andrea was glad to see his home was neat and clean. *He even makes his bed. I wonder if he did that just because I was coming over?*

Mark stepped back to let Andrea in the office first and both gave a sigh of relief to see Muffin on an old, orange sofa sound asleep. She moved to sit by her. "Muffin? You can't just make yourself at home like this!"

"I don't mind." He laughed, "I've spent a lot of time on this couch writing my Kip novels."

Andrea ran her hand over the worn fabric. "It looks umm... well-used. That's for sure."

Mark sat down next to her. "Kip, April and the grandkids love this couch. I've written all of my novels on it and most of the kids sleep here when they come to stay over. I don't know why, but it's always been a good couch."

"I have a chair I rocked my boys in I wouldn't get rid of for love or money."

Settling back to get comfortable, Mark ran his hand along the back of the sofa. "I was saved on this couch."

"Really?" Andrea leaned back, petting Muffin who was still sound asleep.

"Yeah. Mags left me, taking Kip when he was only seven and I was very angry about it." Sighing, Mark admitted, "I was really angry about a lot of things. I drank to forget my pain, but it only brought out the anger I had towards my dad and God."

Andrea didn't speak but listened intently to Mark's story.

Mark continued, "I was angry at my dad for being a violent alcoholic, his abuse of my mom and me, then divorcing her which caused the Catholic church to kick her out, making me mad at God."

Hurting for the young kid angry at God, Andrea reached out to take Mark's hand. He looked at her, a little surprised, "After Mags and Kip left, it took a bit for me to hit rock bottom. Which happened, right after Mags looked at me and said I was acting just as bad as my dad. Well, that was eye-opening."

"It must have been hard to hear."

"That's an understatement. I started going to AA, but found my anger wouldn't abate."

He rubbed his thumb across her hand. "I was trying to work through the steps, but wasn't really getting anywhere. I could admit I had a problem, but couldn't seem to get through step two about a higher power that could help me."

"With what happened with your church, it's understandable."

Relieved she understood, Mark continued to pour out his heart, "I couldn't make myself turn to another higher power, because I did believe in God, I just didn't like Him much. It wasn't until I found a sponsor who encouraged me to go to church, and it helped, because Sundays were the worst for me when I was drinking."

Mark paused, remembering those early days and his friend and sponsor, Charlie Magellan. "Old Charlie Magellan got me into a church and he prayed every day for me to be saved." Mark chuckled, "He said a lot of those prayers out loud to me, too!"

"Magellan..." Andrea paused, thinking a moment, "Wasn't Kip's new ship in the adult series named Magellan?"

Face lighting up, Mark said, "Yeah, it was. I did it to honor Old Charlie. He always bragged about being in one of my novels. He had always been one of my biggest cheerleaders."

"Had?"

"Yeah, Charlie died a few months before we moved here." Mark looked away, picturing old Charlie sitting on this very couch with him, talking about life, love, God, and staying sober.

"I'm so sorry Mark. I can see he meant a lot to you."

"Yeah, he does." He looked back at Andrea. "After a particular sermon, I went to with Charlie, we came back to my place for lunch. We sat on this sofa, while he walked me through asking for forgiveness and helped me to get saved. It's been extra special since that Sunday."

"No wonder, you love this old couch."

Smirking, he pointed. "It's a great couch, just ask Muffin."

She laughed with Mark. "It's a good story." Blushing, she said, "I'm glad you got saved."

"Me, too! It's made a big difference in my life, with Kip and Mags."

Andrea cocked her head, "Did you get saved before you wrote the third Kip adult book?"

Mark's eyes sparkled, "Yes, how did you know?"

Andrea leaned forward a little, "I just remember when I read it, the story seemed different, lighter somehow."

He stared at Andrea, completely amazed by the woman's insight and knowledge. "Wow..." unable to say anything else.

Before either could say more, Mark's cell phone rang and as he picked it up, Andrea glanced at her watch. *Good Lord, it's after eleven. We've been talking for hours. Bailey and Josh are probably wondering what's going on.*

Mark got off the phone. "Sorry about that. It was Kip asking my plans for tomorrow. He has to go into the hospital early, and Becka has a long meeting at church and needs someone to take the kids home after service."

"It's good you're able to do that."

"I wouldn't want it any other way." Mark paused, before asking, "Do you have plans tomorrow after church? Would you like to go to lunch with Noah, Eva and I?"

Andrea's smile stretched from ear to ear, "I'd love that."

"Perfect. I know it's getting late and your family's probably wondering if I've kidnapped you."

Andrea snorted, "They know better, but it is late and we have church tomorrow and lunch with your grandkids."

"Let me see you out."

Mark helped Andrea up, and both laughed as Muffin stood and stretched. "She seems to have gotten in a good nap."

"She's welcome anytime and so are you."

Andrea ducked her head and said thanks, hoping he didn't notice her blushing. After she walked back into the living room to grab her purse and Muffin's favorite chew toy, she turned to say goodbye. "I had a wonderful time."

"Enough to go on another date again, soon?"

"Yes," Andrea whispered as Mark leaned forward.

As he kissed her, Andrea felt the electric shock from her mouth to her toes. *Wow, Lord. What a kisser!*

After a few moments, he leaned back with a lazy smile, "Wow."

Pleased he felt the same way, they each said goodbye and she secretly loved when he walked her to her car and asked her to call him when she made it home.

The drive back to the cottage went quickly as she looked forward to seeing him tomorrow after church.

Mark's Journal Entry – March 1, 2014

Lord,

It's three am and I'm just now laying down for bed. I've been writing since Andrea left a few hours ago. Wow! I'm the most blessed man on this earth to have met this special woman. I could spend the rest of my days kissing her and be content.

After she left, I started to get ready for bed and all of these ideas just came flooding through my mind. I have spent the past four hours writing. If this keeps up, I might make the original deadline for the NOAH story. I can't wait to see Andrea tomorrow and tell her all about what I've written tonight. I took some of the ideas we talked about and incorporated them into the story. I'm hoping she'll read what I've written so far and let me know what she thinks. I'd love to have her opinion, more than just about anyone's at this moment.

I need to get some sleep. I've got church and then the kids tomorrow afternoon. Plus, I'll get to see Andrea and I don't want to yawn through our time together. She's too special!

Thank You, Lord, for tonight's date with Andrea, and for getting me through this writer's block. Please help me to finish this novel on time.

Chapter Eighteen

"I'm here and I've got big news!"

Everyone jumped at the loud banging as Betty Lou came bursting through the classroom door Andrea had reserved for the April widow's meeting.

Beverly moved her purse for Betty to sit by her. "What's your big news?"

"I'm getting married in two weeks!"

The room erupted in questions and comments. Beverly shouted over everyone's loud voices, "When did this happen? Last I knew you'd just gone a few dates!"

Betty sat down, a large smile plastered on her face. "Actually, we've been on quite a few dates these past six months."

One of the other ladies piped up, "Doesn't this seem a little fast?"

"I don't think so, and as Harold says, 'We're not getting any younger.'" Betty, a flush on her cheeks, sneaked a chip off Beverly's plate. "Besides, it's not like we haven't been married before."

"But NOT to each other!"

Amidst the laughter, Betty nodded, "That's true, but Harold and I have had long talks and we know who we are, what we need and want."

Laura Flowers had been quiet through all of the talking, but asked, "And what do you want, Betty?"

Her gray eyes wet with tears, Betty put down the other chip she had stolen. "I want to come home to someone besides my cat every day. I want someone to share the good times and the bad times with for however long God gives me on this earth. I want someone who's kind and makes me laugh, who supports me and encourages me to keep going. I want to be married to Harold and he wants to be married to me. What more can a girl want?"

Several ladies wiped tears, and out of the corner of her eye, Andrea watched Laura duck her head to hide tears of her own. Betty flashed a big smile, "I also want to have someone to cook for. It's so hard to cook for only one person. I don't know how to cut portions and thankfully Harold has a big appetite."

Laughter followed as everyone thought of the skinny doctor who could eat anyone under the table. When it quieted down a bit, Beverly raised her lemonade, "Here's to Betty and Harold. May they be blessed with many happy moments together."

As everyone raised their glasses, Andrea watched Betty tell everyone how Dr. Kline proposed. *She's glowing and happy! She's always been a cheerful lady, but she's like a giddy kid on Christmas.*

"Andrea, Andrea?"

Shaking her head, Andrea turned to Betty. "Sorry."

"I was wondering if you and Bailey would be able to cater a small party after the wedding ceremony?"

"When is the happy day?"

"Friday, April 18th around 7:30." Betty winked. "Harold wants a short ceremony because he has bad knees and doesn't want to do too much standing."

Pulling out her calendar, Andrea looked at it for a moment. "That should be fine. We have the Blake-Toledo wedding this weekend, but nothing the next week. I'll double check with Bales."

"Good." Betty turned to the group, "Of course, you're all invited to the wedding. It will be here at the church and starts at seven. That's why I'm late, I had to discuss details with the pastor."

"Do you have time to meet early next week to discuss the party?"

Betty nodded her head, her large hoop earrings jingling, "Yes. Harold and I can meet you whenever you need Monday or Tuesday."

"Perfect. I'll call you tonight to set up a time."

The rest of the meeting went by quickly after Betty's news, and before long Andrea was rising to help clean up. Finding lids for containers, she backed up and ran into Betty. "Oops, sorry Betty. I didn't see you there. I thought you'd be rushing out to meet Harold. Isn't he waiting for you?"

"Yes, but I wanted to talk to you alone before I left."

"Sure." Wondering what Betty wanted to ask her, Andrea sent up a quick prayer, *Lord, please don't let it be about marriage advice.*

"Well... since I'm getting married in two weeks, I wanted to know if I need to quit attending the widow's group. I mean, I guess I won't be a widow anymore since I'll be remarrying, but well..." Tears in her eyes, Betty whispered, "I don't want to leave. The ladies mean a lot to me... we're friends and I know..."

"Don't you even finish that sentence." Andrea pulled the plump woman into a hug. "Betty Lou Richardson soon to be Mrs. Betty Kline, you're ALWAYS welcome here."

Betty gushed, wiping tears from her eyes, "I was praying you would say that. I wouldn't know what to do if I didn't get to see all of you every month. Each of you has meant so much to me."

Shocked by Betty's reaction, Andrea held onto her hands. "We wouldn't know what to do if you didn't attend and keep us on our toes. You're an inspiration to the group and anyone who knows you, with your cheerful spirit. Your faith in the midst of your circumstances has been a testimony of God's grace. I know when your husband passed away and then your son not even a year later, well, your faith never wavered. I admire you and would truly be hurt if you didn't keep coming to these meetings."

Betty stepped back. "I've never told anyone but Harold... but this group has helped me tremendously. I was in a very bad place when you invited me that first day. I was so lonely and felt God had abandoned me in my old age. It wasn't until you personally invited me to this group, I felt cared for again."

"Betty, I had no idea," Andrea wiped at the tears in her own eyes.

"Well, I was ashamed. As you said, my faith didn't waver when I lost my husband, Joseph and then Bill died not even six months later and I was able to hold firm to my faith, but then I got older and lost my way." Tilting her head, Betty continued, "I had lost my direction and faith. I felt so alone and useless until I started attending these monthly meetings. It was after meeting you I became inspired by how you had moved your whole life across the country, started a new career at fifty, always busy volunteering all over this church... and well watching you, God told me He wasn't finished with me yet. He had a plan and purpose for my life. God renewed my joy, renewed my love for Him, gave me a new purpose. I wouldn't have been able to say yes to Harold's request for the first date if it hadn't been for all of you. I feel like a teenager again!"

"Betty, I wish I had known." Touched by her words, Andrea couldn't believe her life had been an inspiration to anyone, let alone this woman who always seemed happy and cheerful. *Lord, what an eye-opening afternoon this has been... I never knew. Thank You for having me reach out to this sweet lady that Sunday morning. It was Your prompting that I asked her. I thought she was doing so well after her husband died, she could help other ladies in the group... I had no idea what she was going through, but You did!*

It was quiet a moment, before Betty asked, "I was hoping you would be willing to be my matron of honor and stand up with me when I marry Harold."

Her mouth falling open, Andrea stood there unable to speak more than, "Me?"

Nodding her head, Betty's earrings jangled. "Yes! My best friend is in Oregon and won't be able to make the wedding." Betty sniffled, reaching for a Kleenex. "You helped me find my faith again. I'd love to have you stand up beside me."

"Betty, I would be honored to be your matron of honor on your special day."

Hugging the sweet woman, Andrea thought, *Lord, I know there's a lesson in here for me as well. I'm not sure what it is, but I know there is one!*

"Perfect. Well, I need to scoot. Harold and I are going to look at flowers. It will be a simple ceremony but I told him I wouldn't feel right without a bouquet in my hands."

"Be sure to tell us the flowers when we meet next week. I'm sure Bailey will want to incorporate it into the cake."

"Oh good! That girl is so talented. I saw the cake she did the other month and the flowers looked real. I couldn't believe it when she told me they were icing."

"She is gifted. I never cease to be amazed by what she comes up with each time. Every wedding cake is unique and personalized."

"Tell her I can't wait to see what she creates for our special day." Betty picked up her empty container. "I'll see you for Hillary's wedding Saturday. Bill was one of her teachers, and she kindly invited Harold and me."

"I'll see you then."

Saying their goodbyes, Andrea fixed the chairs back for the Sunday School class in a few days. She had just moved to fold up the table when she saw someone walk in the classroom door. "Hi, Andrea. Would you like some help?"

Turning, Andrea saw Mark. A large smile on her face, Andrea said, "Yes, please. What are you doing here?"

"I called the house and Bales said you were here. She mentioned she was picking you up because Josh borrowed your car and I volunteered."

Pleased, she moved forward. "That's nice of you."

Walking up to her, Mark kissed her soundly, "It's not about being nice. I've missed you the last few weeks. Do you mind if I kidnap you for a few hours?"

"No, I don't mind." Andrea blushed.

"I saw Betty Lu downstairs, practically skipping out of here a few minutes ago."

"Yes, well she has a reason, she's getting married in two weeks."

"But she's like eighty!"

"She's only seventy-two."

Chuckling, Mark went back to their original subject. "I got a call this morning. Noah will be pleased to know my editor, David said it was one of my best. He couldn't put it down and had to finish it in one sitting."

She poked his arm. "Told you so! When I read it before you sent it off, I said it was really good."

Mark kissed her again. "You're biased."

"Maybe a little."

Enjoying his playful mood, she realized she had missed him a lot the past month. They had seen each other only once a week while Mark furiously worked on finishing the first draft of the novel. When his writer's block went away, the ideas came in a downpour and he spent most of March speed writing to finish on time. Claiming he had never missed a writing deadline and didn't want to start now, he wrote late into the night.

Andrea wiped off the last table while watching Mark out of the corner of her eye. *I even had to pick up Noah a few times from school because he was in the zone, but I didn't mind at all. I love spending time with Noah.*

"I thought I'd take you with me to pick up Noah and we'd celebrate with ice cream before I dropped you off at home. I know you've got a wedding to cater this Saturday."

"I'd like that. I haven't seen Noah in days. I've missed him."

"Not me?"

"Only a little, I'm really dating you to see Noah."

Mark's laugh was loud and long, as he finished putting up the last table. "I knew it. My famous author charm has worn off and now you only see me to hang out with my grandson."

Snorting, Andrea admitted, "It's true. I'm only dating you to see the little guy."

Mark walked over to put his arm around her. "Then, I'll have to bribe you with a ride in the Aston Martin."

"Then, I'll definitely date you for your car since you're trying to spoil me." Eyes shining bright, she thought, *I know he had to finish his novel quickly and we spent most of our time sitting together on that ugly orange sofa with Muffin snuggled in between as he typed away, bouncing ideas off me. At least this way, we can hold hands again, since he's not typing.*

"You do need a little spoiling, because we started dating and then I abandoned you in almost the same week."

"It's okay. It's been crazy prepping for this wedding and now that Betty's getting married in two weeks, I'll have another wedding party to organize with little time."

"I still can't believe she and Harold are getting married!"

"In two weeks, so Bales and I will have to do a lot the next few days to prepare."

After Mark helped her into the car, Andrea told him everything Betty said while driving to pick Noah up from the elementary school. The two caught up from the last time they had seen each other, a little over a week ago. Holding his hand, Andrea couldn't remember when she felt happier.

"Mrs. Andrea!" Noah yelled while running to the car. "What are you doing here with Grandpa?" He threw his Spiderman backpack into the backseat and grabbed Andrea in a big hug.

"Noah, sit down and buckle up. These soccer moms are giving me dirty looks for holding up the line."

As Noah buckled himself in, Andrea smirked. *Dirty looks, my foot. Every woman who sees him checks him out.* Grinning, she turned to watch Noah squirming in the back seat. *Mark's a handsome, funny guy. He makes me feel safe and special. He looks very dashing in his tweed jacket driving this little sporty convertible.*

"I'm buckled in, Grandpa."

"Good, because we're going to get ice cream to celebrate!"

"Yes." Fist pump in the air, Noah cried out, "What are we celebrating?"

"David called to say he loved the first draft of the NOAH book and thinks we won't have to do too much polishing to have it ready before the end of the year."

"I knew it!"

"Yes, you did, Noah. I'll be meeting him in the next few weeks to start discussing promotion and advertising."

The rest of the ride to Noah's favorite ice cream shop was spent discussing how books are promoted. Noah had lots of ideas for Grandpa's book featuring his name.

When they finally pulled into the store's parking lot, Mark got out of the car and then rushed over to hold the door open for Andrea. "Who needs marketing. I'll just let Noah handle everything. It sounds like he has everything all planned."

The couple laughed when Noah ran up to the counter, but the boy turned quickly toward Mark, "Grandpa, since this is a celebration, can I have sprinkles?"

"Yes, Noah. Sprinkles are definitely needed for a celebration." Mark turned to Andrea, "Butter pecan? Or would you like something else?"

She blushed knowing he remembered. "Yes, a small butter pecan would be perfect."

"Sprinkles?"

"Of course, it's a celebration."

Squeezing her hand before moving to the counter, Mark walked up to place their order. Andrea found a seat while she watched Noah animatedly talking to the ice cream scoop girl about the novel featuring his name. When Mark came to sit, he smiled, "Noah usually doesn't brag so much about me in public. We, Hastings, like our privacy, but he's so excited about this book."

Andrea snorted, "When I met him, he was bragging about you. That boy adores you."

"I don't deserve how blessed I am."

"Do any of us?"

Looking at her brown eyes, Mark marveled at the gold flecks. "No, I guess not, but that little boy makes me feel blessed daily."

Starting to eat her ice cream and Andrea nodded, "I feel the same way."

Noah skipped over to sit with them and told an animated story about his day at school. As Andrea watched the little boy's hands wave back and forth, she thought, *he's just like his grandpa! I wouldn't be surprised if we have another storyteller on our hands.*

The group kept up a lively discussion and much too soon for Mark, all of the ice creams were finished. He crumpled a napkin. "Bud, I think it's time for us to go. You've got homework and I've kidnapped Ms. Andrea long enough."

"Aww, Grandpa. Do we have to leave? My homework won't take long."

"Yes, we do. I won't have your mom getting mad at me for keeping you from your school work."

"But, Grandpa. I've only got a worksheet for math today. It won't take very long at all."

He ruffling his hair. "That's what you said last week and it took us hours to finish it." He turned to Andrea and whispered, "New math is hard."

Andrea nodded, remembering helping her own boys with homework.

"Go throw away the napkins and let's take Ms. Andrea home."

"O...kay."

A sad little boy stood and slowly dragged his feet as he took all the trash to the bin by the door. Mark helped Andrea to stand and held her hand as he walked her to the car. Noah skipped outside, but did a double take when he saw his Grandpa kiss Ms. Andrea on the lips!

Doing a little dance before he got inside, Noah struggled to buckle up. *This is the best thing that could've happened. Phase two of NOAH's plan to unite Grandpa and Ms. Andrea is complete.*

The happy group sang along to the "old people" music on the way to Andrea's house. Pulling into her drive, Noah groaned. *Concentrating on homework now is going to be so hard!*

Chapter Nineteen

"Esta corbata es muy apretada, Papá."

Luke looked over to see his son tugging on his dark blue tie. Hiding a smile, he stooped down to Daniel's level and loosened it slightly. "It's just for the ceremony, Daniel, but we'll loosen the tie just a bit. Then you can take it off like I'm planning to do as soon as the ceremony is over and it's time for food."

Daniel's brown eyes shined. "And then you're married to Ms. Hillary and she's our mom 'ficially?"

He hugged the sweet boy, he now called son. "Yes, then it's official." *And I couldn't be a more blessed man if I tried, Lord.*

"Well, in that case, I guess I can wear this tie a little bit longer."

"Exactly, Daniel. Gentlemen learn to put up with a lot for the women in their lives."

"Really!" Daniel gave a dramatic eye roll.

Luke laughed as they looked into the large mirror to make sure everything was tucked and pressed. Pleased they both looked clean, he picked up Daniel to carry him out of the bathroom. Glancing at his watch, he saw the ceremony would be starting soon. *Let's get this show on the road! I'm ready for Hillary Rachel Blake to become*

Mrs. Hillary Toledo, and I know the kids are more than ready, too! We all can't wait to be a family 'ficially as Daniel says.

"Ready, Luke?"

Luke looked up to see his friend and coworker, Riley Jamison standing in the hallway waiting for them.

"Yes, we are. Daniel wanted a potty break before the boring stuff starts, as he said."

Riley laughed, emphasizing natural lines on his face while running his hand through his short crew cut. "The things we do for our women, Little Man."

"That's what Papá said."

"It's time for us to move to the front. The minister said Hillary was about to make her way down."

"Okay." Setting Daniel down, Luke asked, "Who has Camilla?"

"My wife. She's sitting in the front row so Camilla can see you both."

"Perfect." Taking a deep breath, Luke prayed, *Lord, thank You for bringing Hillary into my life. She'll be a wonderful wife and mother to our kids.*

Moving to the front of their home church in Marietta, Luke looked out at the small crowd and was touched so many of their friends and family were in attendance. He and Hillary had both wanted a small wedding and most importantly, they wanted it to be kid-friendly. The short ceremony was to be early in the morning followed by a brunch reception before the two of them went off on their honeymoon. They were to stay in a cute bed and breakfast until Monday afternoon, before the entire Blake, Diego, and Toledo clan went on a spring break vacation to St. Augustine Beach, Florida. The kids had never been to the beach and with all the grandparents along, he and Hillary would be able to have some alone time, too. They were renting a huge condo to accommodate the large clan.

The sanctuary grew quiet as the parents were escorted down the aisle. Diego and Ana Sophia were stepping in since they had been like grandparents to him. He knew his own mother was looking down from Heaven with a smile on her face. *She would've loved Hillary, almost as much as I do.*

Shortly after they were seated, Lauren Blake walked down the aisle. Luke smiled at his future mother-in-law and sent up another prayer of thanks for how much Lauren had changed in the last few months. He couldn't believe how much he had grown to love Hillary's mother and father. Alex and Lauren had become the parents he had lost after his father abandoned them and his mother died of cancer when he was in high school.

Soon the only bridesmaid started walking down the aisle and Luke winked at Ivy Ingles, Hillary's best friend from college. He would always be grateful to the young woman because she was the one who told Hillary of his desperate need for a nanny and the rest was history.

When he glimpsed Magda walking down the aisle in a pretty blue ball gown that matched Hillary's eyes, his chest swelled with love for the little girl, his niece now daughter. She had truly blossomed the past few months. The birthday party Hillary organized for February fourteenth was for a different girl than the one he first met, scared and hungry, lost without her mother.

The party had been large with all of her friends from church and classmates invited. Their little Magda was quite the social butterfly now and made friends easily. He winked at Magda as she moved to stand by Ivy and the giggle, she sent him warmed his heart. *It's hard to believe she's the same little girl.*

Distracted for a moment, he turned back to face the doors when he saw everyone stand. His breath caught in his chest at the first glimpse of his bride-to-be. Hillary stood at the end of the aisle, arm in arm with her tall father. Alex Blake was beaming at her and Luke couldn't help feeling honored this special woman loved him. *She's beautiful inside and out, but this morning, she's radiant.*

Hillary started walking slowly down the aisle, and Luke had to tell himself to breathe. Hillary had told him a few months ago, when she and her mother had gone to Grace's dress shop, that it was while shopping for her wedding dress she knew her mother had truly changed. Instead of picking out her wedding dress and telling Hillary what to wear, Lauren had pulled a few dresses and let Hillary try on the ones she wanted, even options Lauren didn't pick herself.

Crying as she told Luke the story later that night, she said her mother did not say one negative thing to her about any of the dresses. Each one she tried on was beautiful on her, just not the one. When Hillary said she picked a simple V-neck sheath dress, her mother had cried saying it was perfect, even when it was one Hillary had found.

Luke had no clue what she meant by that description, but seeing her walk down the aisle in an ivory dress with a small train, he knew she had picked the perfect dress. Hillary said she was prepared to do battle to pick the gown she wanted and couldn't be happier she didn't even have to stand up for herself, because her mother stood in support of her.

Alex put Hillary's hand in his after the minister asked who gave this woman before the father of the bride went to sit by his teary wife. Luke looked into Hillary's eyes and saw his future reflected in the crystal blue depths.

The ceremony was short and sweet, and after vows and the rings, the Pastor said, "You may now kiss the bride."

Amidst shouts and yells, Luke took Hillary into his arms and kissed her soundly. They echoed in their hearts, *finally*!

Turning to face the crowd, the happy couple beamed as the pastor announced, "I'm proud to introduce Mr. and Mrs. Luke Toledo."

Hillary and Luke walked down the aisle arm in arm and made their way to the back of the lobby. They stood there waiting as Daniel and Magda came rushing down the aisle to leap into their waiting arms. "Mamá," Magda cried, her arms wrapped tightly around Hillary's neck.

"I'm so happy, Ladybug."

Looking into her new daughter's eyes, Hillary thanked God for this family she was now a part of. The plan was for her to officially adopt the kids as Luke had done in December. Paperwork was all filled out and now she was officially married to their dad, it would just be going before a judge to make it 'ficial as Daniel said.

"Cake, now?" Daniel piped up.

Luke tousled his dark hair, "Soon. But first, pancakes."

"But they're not Mamá's pancakes."

Hillary laughed at her son. "No, but they are Bailey's, which I think are just as good, if not better."

Daniel shook his head vigorously, "No way, Mamá. Your pancakes are the best!"

Picking up his son, Luke turned to his family. "That's only because you went from my yucky pancakes straight to Hillary's heavenly ones."

The family laughed over the funny story as they made their way to the reception hall. Hillary had told Andrea they wanted to have a few minutes alone with Daniel and Magda before the reception started. Walking to the fellowship hall, they were all stunned by the decorations Taste & See Catering had set up for the reception.

Spying them, Andrea walked over to the new family. "Do you like it?"

Hillary had tears in her eyes. "It's simply stunning. I had no idea…"

Luke turned to the older woman. "I have no words. How?"

"It was Lauren's idea actually. She thought a fairy tale reception with all of the white Christmas lights would be a surprise for the kids."

"I'm going to mess up my makeup again." Hillary put her head on Luke's shoulder. Looking down at Magda and Daniel who could only look around with their mouths hanging open, Hillary whispered, "Where did you get all the lights? There must be thousands!"

Andrea chuckled, "Closer to a half million. Your mom reached out to both churches and your school to have people bring their white lights. She said when your new family got to the fellowship hall, she wanted you to know each light represents a prayer for all of you."

Tears in her own eyes, Andrea watched the family in such awe. *I thought Lauren's idea was brilliant but didn't know how we'd get all the lights to pull it off. That sweet woman took care of it, and was here late last night with a group of volunteers stringing lights. I told her we could do it, but she insisted on doing this for her daughter's future family. It was worth it!*

Grateful Viviane had snuck behind them to take pictures of the kids rushing toward their parents for the first time, she had been able to capture their reaction in seeing the fellowship hall turned fairyland. People started arriving from the other end of the church and their astonishment was just as strong as the new family's own awe.

Andrea helped the new couple get each of the kids a plate of food. She knew the plan was to let the kids eat a bit and then take family pictures. The party was in full swing and Andrea spent the next hour busily directing and filling glasses.

"It looks amazing, Andrea."

Turning, Andrea saw Lauren Blake arm in arm with her husband walking up to them. "I'm telling you, Lauren, you missed a calling. This reception space is stunning and it had nothing to do with my talents."

Lauren stepped forward to hug her. "Nonsense. I only hung lights. You did EVERYTHING else and it's amazing. I've been eating your daughter's pancakes like a starving woman."

"They are delicious. I just can't figure out what Bailey put in the pancake mix." Alex rubbed his belly.

"Some sort of tea mix Bales knew Hillary loves."

Alex slapped his forehead, "Of course. I thought it smelled familiar."

"I was unsure when she mentioned the idea to me, especially since Luke and Hillary stressed kid-friendly, but Bales was right of course and they are divine."

Mark walked up at that moment and chimed in, "Bailey's a genius in the kitchen that's for sure." Speaking directly to the Blakes, he continued, "Sorry to steal her from you, but she's needed in the kitchen for a moment."

Lauren hugged her. "Tell Bailey for me I want the recipe because it's amazing."

Andrea stepped away. "I'll tell her and make sure she emails it to you."

Following Mark toward the kitchen, she stopping occasionally to tuck this or move that. Leaving the open reception area, Andrea asked, "Is something wrong? I thought Bailey had everything under control when I left. Josh was in the kitchen helping her."

"Everything's fine. I just wanted to do this."

Mark leaned forward and kissed her, enjoying the blush that covered her cheeks. After a few moments, he reluctantly let her go. "And Bailey did have a question about something. I just volunteered to get you because I wanted to start my payment early for helping."

She snorted. "We weren't that desperate for help. Just because almost all of our normal servers are away for spring break..."

"Pluh-lease. You were begging for help the other day. Josh and I felt sorry with all the bribing you and Bales were doing to get volunteers. We decided to help out because we are true gentlemen."

Arching an eyebrow, Andrea waved her hand at him. "Oh please, we both know you can't stand to be away from me." She danced away from him and called over her shoulder, "I'm going to have to work harder to keep some distance from you. I can't have you become infatuated with me."

Mark watched her dance off to check on Bales and said quietly to the empty hallway, "A little too late."

Chapter Twenty

"Can I please get everyone's attention?"

Everyone looked over to see Alex Blake standing at the front with his wife, Lauren smiling sweetly by his side. "Hillary and Luke will be leaving soon, but my lovely bride and I," Alex said while sliding his arm around his wife, "wanted to give Hillary, Luke, and our three grandkids their wedding present before the couple leaves for their honeymoon."

Hillary looked up from the table she was sitting at with Luke and the kids. She was feeding Camilla a few bites of pancake while Daniel and Magda were munching on their second round, which Daniel declared were almost as good as his mamá's cooking.

She arched an eyebrow at Luke, who only shrugged before she turned to face her parents once again. *They're up to something, I can tell.*

With a beaming smile, Alex winked at Hillary. "It's not every parent that's blessed with such a loving and sweet daughter."

Hillary felt herself blushing, but focused on her father's words. "Hillary's biggest theme for this wedding was simple, but elegant which between her, my wife, and Taste & See Catering succeeded beyond measure."

Clapping for the group of talented women was loud and long before Alex was able to continue, "My wife and I had set aside an amount of money for her wedding day and my sweet girl didn't even use a quarter of it. After talking with each other and running our idea by Luke, we wanted to present the family with our wedding gift."

Hillary's eyes jerked to her new husband, noticing the sly grin across his handsome face. *I knew it*! Seeing he still wasn't going to give her any hints, Hillary turned back to the front.

Alex and Lauren walked over to the newlyweds and put a piece of paper in Luke's outstretched hands. Alex took Hillary in his arms. "We've taken the money from your wedding fund and put a down payment on the house you and Luke will be living in. This way you don't have to keep renting and looking for another."

Lauren kissed her daughter with tears in her eyes. "My grandbabies only know that house as their home and we know how much work you and Luke have put into it. Please accept this gift."

She cut her eyes to Luke, and said quickly, "We discussed this with Luke before we set it in motion. I didn't want you to think we were control..."

Hillary didn't let her mom finish, but threw her arms around Lauren. "Oh, Mom. Thank you and Dad both. This is the most wonderful present, perfect for us as a family." Tears welling in her eyes, she hugged both of her parents. "Thank you!"

"Does this mean we don't have to move houses?"

Lauren looked down at Magda, her heartstrings tugged by these sweet kids. *Lord, how could I not have loved them at first sight.* Scooping up the little girl, she nuzzled her cheek. "No sweetie, you and your siblings are in your very own home."

Magda wrapped her tiny arms around her abuela's neck. "Good, because we like that casa."

Alex picked up Daniel with a chuckle. "We know kiddos and we wanted to make sure you didn't have to move out of it."

Luke shook Alex's hand. "Thank you, sir."

"It's Dad, Luke. I'd be honored for you to call me Dad."

Luke's eyes became a bit blurry. "Thank you, Dad."

Lauren coughed. "Luke, I know you had a wonderful mother, but I'd be honored if you would call me Mom."

Hugging the woman, he had grown to love over the past few months, Luke said, "I'd love that, Mom!"

The family hugged and then Alex said, "It's time for you two to get going. We'll take the kids and get in line to wave you off."

Saying their goodbyes, Hillary hugged each of the kids and then her dad. "Thank you, Daddy. I've been truly blessed having you as a father. You've encouraged me to be the woman you're so proud of and I can never thank you enough for that."

Tearing up, Alex hugged his baby girl, "Thank you, Baby Girl," was all he could say, but he prayed, *Lord, it's hard to let her go, but it's a comfort to know she's going with a good man. Plus, Lauren and I got three of the most precious grandkids out of the deal.*

Finished saying goodbye to her father, Hillary turned to her mother. Lauren walked up to embrace her. "I'm so proud of you, my daughter. You're going to be a wonderful wife and mother."

"Thank you, Mom. I can't tell you how much that means to me."

Tearing up again, Lauren grabbed her twentieth tissue of the morning, "Well, it's true. I'm just sorry it's taken so long for me to tell you."

Hillary hugged her mother. "The important thing is you did tell me and I'm so proud to call you my mom."

Lauren really started to cry. "You need to scoot. You can't keep Luke waiting. We've got the kids at our house until Monday afternoon and then we'll meet you at your house to leave for spring break."

Hillary straightened up, and said, "I know the kids are so excited about the beach." Hillary leaned forward quickly and said, "Truth be told, I think Ana Sophia and Diego are just as excited."

"It will be a great family trip, now scoot." Sending her off, Lauren called after her, "Oh, and don't forget the bag I packed for you. I set it in the room where you were getting ready this morning."

Hillary rushed to change and touch up her makeup just a bit from all of the crying this morning. *Tears of joy, Lord. Tears of joy.*

Rounding the hall, she saw Christy Boulier walking by. "Hi, Christy!"

Hugging her newly married friend, Christy fell in step with her. "You're a beautiful bride, Hillary Toledo."

"Thank you, I'm never going to get tired of hearing that!" Hillary said, "I haven't had a chance to say anything more than hello this morning."

"It has been a big day for you."

The two friends started giggling as they walked into the classroom Hillary used to get ready this morning. "I've got to touch up my makeup and grab the bag my mom packed, but I'm not sure where it is."

"I'll look. You fix your makeup."

"Thanks."

"Oh, wait, before you do. I have this card for you."

Hillary paused to open it and as she read, the tears began to fall again. "Christy? Oh, this is a perfect wedding present."

Hugging the small brown-haired woman, Hillary grabbed a tissue. "The kids will be thrilled."

"Well, your mother mentioned they were putting your wedding money toward the home you and Luke had been working on and several of us wanted to do something special for all of you."

"I think re-decorating the kid's rooms to fit their personalities will be so special. You've babysat enough to know what each of them loves."

"Yes, I have plenty of volunteers to help paint while your family is on vacation/honeymoon this week. Your third-grade class helped paint furniture and created artwork to hang in Camilla's bedroom until she's older and can decide how to make it her own."

"Christy..." Hillary couldn't even finish, she was crying so hard. "Thank you." *How sweet my classroom helped with the decorating! I'll need to make sure to tell Camilla when she gets older and can understand.*

"Well," the woman blushed. "I knew your class and friends would want to do something special and everyone knows how much you love your new family and well..."

Hugging her friend since high school, Hillary said, "You couldn't have chosen a better gift. It's so sweet of you to use your design skills to give my kids beautiful bedrooms. Luke painted each room, but the furniture was old and secondhand."

"Well, everyone will be surprised when you get back from the beach next weekend."

"Do you have a key?"

"Yes, your mom gave me one."

Touching up her makeup, Hillary talked ideas with Christy about the kids' rooms. The young woman's talent for design was evident in her plans. Shortly, Andrea poked her head in the door, "Are you ready, Hillary? Everyone's lined up and Luke looks anxious."

Hillary laughed, "He hates being the center of attention. It's one of the many reasons he wanted the kids so involved in the wedding."

Taking the bag from Christy, Hillary took a deep breath, "I'm ready."

Andrea fixed a stray lock of hair. "Yes, you are. Have a wonderful honeymoon and vacation with your family."

"Thank you, Andrea." Hugging her friends, Hillary gushed, "The wedding was perfect. Thank you for all of your help. Tell Bales I said thank you, too!"

"I will. Now hurry."

As they watched her run off, Andrea sighed before turning to Christy. "Christy, I wanted to ask a favor."

"Sure, Andrea."

"Mark volunteered to take the leftovers from the wedding to Harvest House, and while I love the man, he can't find places without help. His sense of direction is horrible."

Christy giggled, "I understand. It's a running joke in my family I can't find a place unless I've eaten there."

"I remember you saying that once. I thought since Harvest House is a part of your church, you could drive back to Cartersville and show him the way on your way home."

"Sure. That's not a problem."

"I'd do it, but we'll be cleaning up here for a bit."

"I can help unload, too. That way it will take half the time."

"You're a dear." Andrea led the young woman to the kitchen. "Mark has to be back in town this afternoon for Noah's soccer practice tonight, which is why I'm sending him on now. I'll introduce you and then you can both leave when you're ready."

The door to the kitchen opened, and they heard Bailey shout, "Josh, you're loading this dishwasher wrong!"

"But, it's not the dishwasher at home. We're just washing a few of the churches things we borrowed. They don't have a system here. There isn't a diagram, I checked."

Andrea chuckled as she whispered, "It's their ongoing argument. I think Josh only loads it to get a rise out of her. He knows he always does her special system wrong. She even drew out a special diagram and posted it on the fridge and HE STILL gets it wrong. I'm starting to think it's on purpose."

To prevent anymore arguing, Andrea called loudly, "Mark? I found Christy and she has graciously volunteered to lead you to Harvest House."

"Andrea, my dear, I told you I can find it on my own." Mark came over while drying a large bowl.

"And make it on time to Noah's soccer practice, I don't think so."

"Now, dear..." he threw the towel over his shoulder.

Christy chuckled to herself to see the older couple fussing just like the younger one. *Just over a different subject.*

"You got us completely lost last week when we went to see Noah's soccer game in Marietta."

"But I had never been before..." he protested.

"Exactly! You haven't driven to Harvest House before either. Usually, Josh and Bales drop off the leftovers, but I need Josh to help take down the lights."

"Just admit defeat, Mark," Josh placed another plate in the wrong spot. *There's no diagram here.* He smirked, "Mom always gets her way."

Bailey moved behind Josh to move the plate to the correct spot and called out, "He's right for once, Mark. Andrea's going to win this argument."

Mark winked at Andrea, before turning to Christy. "Hi, I'm Mark Hastings."

Taking his outstretched hand, Christy whispered, "I know who you are, Mr. Hastings. I've read all of your novels. I've enjoyed sci-fi since I was little and yours are some of the best."

"Please, it's Mark. Fans like you can call me by my first name."

"Mark, Christy is also a writer." Andrea piped up.

"Really? That's wonderful."

Blushing, Christy waved her hands, "Oh, not really. I've written one book, but I'm nowhere near your level. I'm still deciding what to do about the whole publishing thing."

"We all have to start somewhere, my dear." He picked up a container of food. "If you'd ever like to meet and talk writing, let me know. It's always good to have more writer friends."

Christy's eyes widened, "Thank you! I'll take you up on it."

He leaned forward to whisper, "It's the least I can do for someone helping me get where I need to be. I can't admit it to Andrea, but I'll never find this place on my own and make Noah's game on time."

"I'm happy to help. Harvest House is a place close to my heart. It's wonderful Andrea and Bailey donate leftovers from their events to help feed the Bartow County community."

"My girlfriend's a sweet woman that's for sure."

It didn't take long for the leftovers to be packed up in Mark's jeep. Christy enjoyed spending time with the two couples, and as she ran to her car so Mark could follow her to Harvest House, she wondered, *does Andrea know she said she loved Mark?*

Chapter Twenty-One

"I think I'm going to be sick."

"Betty, are you okay?" Andrea walked over to stand by Betty who was looking a little green, the same color as Andrea's matron of honor dress.

"What was I thinking? Getting married again at my age. For goodness sake, I'm seventy-two years old! I must be crazy."

Taking a piece of paper to fan the older woman, Andrea steered her to a chair, and gently pushed her into a sitting position. "It's okay, Betty. I think it's just nerves."

Tears welling up in her eyes, Betty asked, "Do you think I'm crazy?"

Stooping down to be eye level, Andrea took Betty's hand and said, "No, dear, I don't think you're crazy. I think you're just a bit nervous because it's a big change, but I've seen you with Harold and you're perfect for each other."

A sweet smile on her face, asked, "Really?" She blushed. "He is a nice man."

"Yes, he is. Your Harold's kind, funny, and most importantly absolutely adores you!"

Betty looked down at her new engagement ring. "Yes, he does. I feel cherished when I am with him."

"Exactly. Hold on to that feeling and you'll feel much better."

She took a deep breath, "Thank you! I knew having you as my matron of honor was a wise decision."

"I'm honored you asked me." Andrea plucked a tissue from the box. "Now wipe your eyes and let's get you two married. The ceremony should be starting soon and we need to get you to the sanctuary doors for your grand entrance."

Betty stood and looked in the full-length mirror. She noticed the lines and wrinkles on her face that weren't there the last time she said I do. She wore a simple blue dress because it was Harold's favorite color. Satisfied, Betty turned to pick up the bouquet of lilies Andrea held out for her. *I can do this, and more importantly, I want to do this. Ready or not, Harold, here I come!*

Smoothing her dress, she turned to Andrea, "I'm ready. Let's get married."

Andrea saw the determination and peace in the woman's eyes and knew it was going to be all right. Arm in arm, the two ladies walked to the sanctuary entrance to meet her grandson who would give her away when she went down to meet Harold. When the music started, Andrea moved forward to walk slowly down the aisle before the bride and smiled to see all of Betty's friends and family there to support the sweet couple.

Lord, I don't know if I'd want a big to do like this if I remarried. I know this is a simple wedding, but it is still a bit too formal for my liking.

Walking slowly to a Frank Sinatra song, Andrea glanced over to see Mark had snuck in the back to see her walk down the aisle. She sent him a wink, before focusing on her steps.

Mark watched her slowly make her way down and thought to himself, *she's the prettiest woman in the room. I'm a blessed man, Lord.*

Once the Pastor started the ceremony, Mark walked back to the kitchen to finish the last-minute prep for the party starting soon. He knew Harold made it clear he wanted a fast ceremony. The old man had said at the rehearsal dinner last night he wasn't wasting any more time to marry his lovely bride to be.

Picturing Andrea in her simple, long green dress walking down the aisle, he sighed. *Harold might have the right idea.*

Opening the double doors, he looked over at Bailey. "What can I do to help?"

Wiping her forehead with the back of her hand, Bailey smiled. "The ice needs to be set out and then I think we're good to go."

"I'll get right on it. The ceremony started, so the guests should be arriving soon."

"It was so sweet of you to volunteer to help, especially since Josh couldn't because he had a work meeting in Atlanta tonight."

"I don't mind, because it means spending more time with Andrea. How could I not volunteer?"

As he walked off, Bailey smiled. *He's a good man. I'm so glad he and Andrea worked things out. It has been so nice seeing the two of them together the past few months. Andrea positively glows when he's in the room and Mark spends his time watching her every move with a large smile plastered on his face.*

Soon guests started to arrive and Mark was kept busy handing out drinks. *I know Andrea's probably taking group photos right now, but I'll feel better when I can see her. She's been very quiet the past few days and I'm a little worried about her.*

Twenty minutes later, he let out a big sigh when he saw her coming around the corner holding Betty's bouquet as the happy couple was introduced to all of the guests as husband and wife. He soon lost track of her as the celebration kicked into full gear and he spent the next hour working his tail off. Mark tried to catch her eye a few times throughout the night, but the crowd was constantly standing in his line of sight.

Helping another lady, refill her plate, he mused, *Bailey tried to warn me, but I thought she was exaggerating about this crew. I mean half the guests are in their seventies and they're more active than the younger crowd. These people are making ME feel old and behind the times.*

"Laura, are you okay?" Catching up with the woman, rushing to leave, Andrea saw the tears in her friend's eyes and was worried.

Turning to face her friend, Laura whispered, "Yes, I'm fine. I just need to pick up Brian. He's at Noah's house and I don't want to keep him out too late. He had a cold earlier this week and I want him to rest some this weekend."

"I know Betty's glad you came."

A wistful smile on her face, Laura watched the happy couple twirling on the dance floor. "I wouldn't miss it for the world. It was a sweet ceremony. Their vows had me tearing up."

Andrea hugged the young woman and sent up a prayer. *She looks as tired as I feel, but now isn't the time to ask about her about why she's really tearing up.* She turned to go find Bailey when she felt someone touch her arm.

"Mrs. Andrea?"

She turned to see Dr. Kline in his dark suit smiling at her, his grin stretching from ear to ear. She smiled back at the older gentleman. "Hello, Dr. Kline. I thought you'd be with your bride."

"I was but wanted to take a moment to say thank you, dear. Betty Lu told me you calmed her down before the ceremony and I wanted to thank you for encouraging that sweet woman to say yes to my request for a date. I'd been trying to ask her out for months when one Sunday she walked up to me and said yes, before I even said good morning. I wouldn't be here married to my Betty if it weren't for you."

Blushing, Andrea ducked her head, muttering, "Oh, I didn't do anything really."

Clearing his throat, the older gentleman nodded his bald head vigorously. "Yes, you did and I'm very grateful."

Hiding a yawn, Andrea blushed a deeper shade of red. "I'm sorry. I haven't been sleeping well the past few days."

"Oh, my dear. You should know sleep deprivation can be a sign of serious health issues." Twisting his bow tie, Dr. Kline continued, "It can mean diabetes, sleep apnea, or even glandular fever!"

Good Lord! "Now, Doctor. I'm fine, just sleepy. Oh look, Betty's waving you over. I think you two are leaving soon for your honeymoon."

Straightening his bowtie again, Dr. Kline rose to his full height of five foot six. "Well, I can't keep my bride waiting. We're going to the Bahamas on a cruise."

He started to walk away but came back after he pulled a card out of his breast pocket. "My son's an excellent doctor and I'm sure he could fit you in for a full checkup next week. Ron was my best man and one of the top doctors in the county."

Andrea took the card and said, "Thank you." *I wonder if the son is like his father? They both were wearing bowties today.*

As he rushed off, Andrea walked to the kitchen in her second attempt to check on Bailey.

"Andrea, sweetheart. Are you okay?"

She looked up to see Mark walking over to her. *Bailey's going to think I've abandoned her tonight.* "I'm fine. Just a little tired. I haven't been able to sleep well the last few nights." Seeing the worry in his eyes, she said quickly, "It's probably because I've been worried about standing up with Betty for the wedding."

"You've been a bit quiet for the past few days and I'm pretty sure it isn't because of the wedding."

Andrea leaned against the wall and sighed. "I got a letter from Jacob on Wednesday."

"Oh? Is he all right?"

Nodding, tears filled her eyes. "It was a short, handwritten note to say he was fine, but his current assignment meant he didn't have access to a computer." Tears flowing, she softly cried, "It was ONLY three sentences."

"I'm sorry, sweetheart." Wrapping his arms around her, he held her tight while she sobbed into his shoulder.

"We've never gone this long without talking. I haven't heard his voice since last September."

Mark rubbed her back. "Well, at least now you know he's okay and thinking of you."

Sniffling, Andrea said into his shoulder, "Yes, that's true."

"Besides, he's in God's capable hands. You've got the church, your family, and mine praying for his safety."

Andrea only nodded her head, unable to lift her head from his shoulder.

Mark continued, "Noah prayed for him just the other night when I was there to tuck him in."

Lifting her head, Andrea wiped at the tears in her eyes, "He did?"

He leaned closer, kissing the tip of her nose. "He did. I know for a fact he asks for prayer specifically for Jacob each week in Sunday school class, plus Kip and Becka are praying, too! Your son's covered in prayer."

Andrea threw her arms around him, "Thank you for reminding me God has my son in His hands. I love you."

They both froze at Andrea's words. She stepped back as she felt the blush rising to her cheeks until Mark leaned forward to take her hands. "I love you, too, Andrea

Cabot. I think you're the most wonderful thing to happen to me since I held my grandkids in my arms."

As he bent down to kiss her, Andrea felt loved all the way down to her toes. *I do love this man, Lord!*

"Andrea, are you here?"

Andrea stepped back from Mark to see Bailey standing in the hall, a big serving spoon in her hands.

Bailey seeing them in each other's arms, waved the spoon. "Oh, so... sorry. I wanted to see if you could pack the cake for the couple to take home." Blushing, Bailey started backing away. "Harold and Betty are getting ready to leave."

"Yes, of course."

Andrea turned to Mark. "I'm not done with this conversation, yet. Do you want to drive me home after we're done?"

"I'd love, too!"

He watched her march to the fellowship hall with a bit of pep in her step to pack up the little cake Bailey made for the couple to eat on their one-year anniversary. *Lord, it looks like Harold does have the right idea.*

Mark's Journal Entry – April 18, 2014

Lord,

It's late but I wanted to write down my thanks for tonight. I've been wanting to tell Andrea I love her for a few weeks now but was scared she might think it was too soon. Betty Lu and Harold's wedding showed me I shouldn't wait, time was precious. Then surprise! Andrea went ahead and said it first.

I couldn't believe it, but I felt I was ten feet tall when the words came rushing out of her mouth. I know she said it without thinking, but it felt so right to hold her and say the words right back. There was no hesitation.

I do love her and I'm glad I was able to comfort her tonight. I know she's worried about Jacob and I can't imagine how hard it must be to have a son in harm's way when you don't even know where he is or what's he's doing, just it's dangerous. I worry about my kids and grandkids and we're all in the same city.

When I dropped her off tonight, I saw Josh as I was leaving and told him about Jacob's message. I know he left to go talk to her as well. He hadn't known but was glad I told him. It's important to me he knows I want to be there for all of them.

I was honored when Josh ran back to hug me and say thanks for looking out for his mom. She raised some wonderful boys and I'm blessed to be a part of their family's lives. Please continue to protect Jacob and give his mom a peace that passes all understanding.

Chapter Twenty-Two

"Door's open, Michael."

Michael opened the kitchen door and after wiping his feet walked into the kitchen. "Good morning, ladies."

He walked over to the large island where the two women were prepping for another catering event in the afternoon. "The guys are working on the painting and flooring, but I wanted to give you an update on the progress since you're both here. We were delayed after the extensive women's bathroom changes."

"Yes, I know it was a big change at the last minute," Andrea paused while decorating cookies, "but I think it will be a big hit with the women who attend events at Taste & See Catering."

Michael smirked, "When I mentioned the delay it was causing to my wife, she said it was a brilliant idea and told me I should be glad to be working on such an innovative idea." Looking sheepish, he continued, "I was a bit worried it was going to mess up the June first deadline, but it really hasn't caused much of a delay like I was afraid it would."

"I thought Mom was crazy when she mentioned it, too," Bailey agreed, flour up to her elbows. "But the more I thought about doubling the occupancy in the ladies' restrooms and having a small sitting area I knew it was actually just another brilliant idea of Andrea Cabot."

Andrea blushed, "Oh, you two! I just thought of all of the events I've attended over the years with women waiting forever in line for the bathroom, often missing out on the main event, and I don't want that to happen at any of our gatherings."

"So, Michael, how's everything going?" Bailey asked, "I know you guys have been working extra hard to get it done in time for the wedding we have scheduled June seventh."

"Yes, and that's why I wanted to tell you the good news myself. We're scheduled to be done on May 29. It will give you a little over a week to set up for the wedding."

Andrea clapped her hands, "That's wonderful and much sooner than we had hoped." She turned to Bailey. "It's a fitting time to be done because it's also the one-year anniversary of the day we became partners."

"It is!" A big smile crossed her face, as Bailey gushed, "I think this calls for a party to celebrate our anniversary and the opening of the new buildings. Taste & See has grown so much in the last year, we need to celebrate."

"You just love an excuse to party."

"I really do." Bailey turned to Michael. "You and your whole family will be invited, of course. We couldn't have done this without you, especially changing the structural plans at the last minute. Your crew has been amazing."

The large, former football player actually started to blush, when Andrea added, "It's true and the new building you've added is absolutely stunning. Bales and I couldn't be more pleased with how everything turned out."

"Well... I umm... it was your designs and ideas, I just built it."

"Nonsense," Andrea flicked of her hand, "You and your men did a wonderful job. Please tell them they are invited, too!"

"I'll do that. They've all loved the great food they've received while working this job. I know many of them will be sad once we're through." His loud booming laugh echoed through the kitchen, "I can't tell you how many of my guys have put on weight during this job, and that's very hard to do when our work is as physical as it is!"

Bailey and Andrea joined in the laughter. Bailey moved to mix more cookies. "They've made wonderful testers for my pastries and cakes. After a while, Josh starts to look a little green when I give him too many sweets to try. I've gotten such good insight based on the construction crew's taste buds."

After he left still laughing, Andrea and Bailey started to make plans for the party.

"We'll need to invite former clients..."

"Oh, people from our church like the Sunday school class ladies, both pastors, and their families," Andrea quickly added.

"And we should invite Mark's family."

Andrea blushed, grabbing her notebook from her purse on the counter. "Yes, and the widow's group." Knowing Bailey had new food ideas to try out, she asked, "What type of food were you thinking for this shindig?"

Pausing to mix the cake batter she was making, Bailey wiped her hands. "Something simple to serve. We don't want to spend the whole anniversary party serving everyone."

"Maybe a buffet of some type? Any ideas you want to test out on a group for a future event?"

"Hmm... I've been thinking about an international theme. It would let me try out a bunch of different types of food all at once. I've got a whole list of recipes I want to test on you and Josh, between now and then."

"That sounds perfect." Pen in her mouth, Andrea mused, "We will need music. Now that we have the big dance floor, we need to use it."

"Genius. I'll talk to Malcolm and see if his cousin wants to DJ the event. He was excellent at the last wedding we did." Bailey moved to hug Andrea. "I'm so thankful Preston replaced me and made me so mad I came down here to get away from him and start over. It's the best decision I've ever made."

Andrea hugged her friend, business partner, and daughter-in-law all wrapped in one. "It was a God-timed moment for both of us. I still can't believe how much life has changed in just a year."

Laughing, Bailey said, "It's amazing how well it's all worked out. A year ago, I never thought I'd be married to your son, planning a big party to celebrate our partnership, and already expanding the business. It definitely wasn't a part of my plan, but thankfully it was a part of God's."

"It is crazy how much the business has grown. If we hadn't started the plans to build on when we did, we'd be in a pickle right now."

"God's timing..." Bailey winked as Andrea finished, "Is perfect!"

The two ladies laughed before they started to plan in detail the one-year anniversary party in less than twenty-eight days. They had a lot to do in between the standing catering appointments for the month of May. It would be a very busy month.

Andrea couldn't believe it had already been a year, and how many things had changed in her life. Mixing up the last batch of cookies, she mused. *Look at me, Lord. I'm fifty-one, celebrating an anniversary with a new business and excited to meet my boyfriend later tonight for a movie at his house. Though, I think he wants my ideas about the editing suggestions from his editor. I remember being so angry about the car accident taking me away from catering with Bailey in the way we had planned, but if the accident hadn't happened, I wouldn't have met Noah and then his sweet grandfather.*

<u>Mark's Journal Entry - May 1, 2014</u>

Lord,

I just got off the phone with Josh. I think his idea to take Bailey and Andrea out to celebrate their special anniversary is a smart idea. We're going to meet tomorrow at the local coffee shop to discuss ideas of how to celebrate. We both want to do something extra special for them. As Josh said, the party they're planning will be a lot of work, and his idea to do something special for just the two of them to relax and enjoy is brilliant.

I've been working on my manuscript the past week to finish the edits my editor sent me and will enjoy the break. I'm not sure yet what we can do, but I know Josh wants to do something a little over the top. I think he has the right idea!

Andrea told me how badly Josh reacted to the business when she first started it and then when Bailey came on board, things between her and Josh became strained because he was vehemently against both Bailey and the catering business. I think this is Josh's way to make up for it, and I couldn't be more excited to help. I should get to bed. We're meeting early in the morning because I want to pick up Noah from school that afternoon and need to get the last of the edits done before I do.

When Andrea came over this evening, her insights into David's comments about the novel were spot on. It shouldn't still amaze me how insightful my Andrea is. I think this last draft will be completed soon and I can start thinking about my next novel. I've got a few ideas floating around, but I'm interested to see what Andrea thinks.

"So, you agree?"

Mark took another sip of his coffee before replying, "Yes. I think it's perfect. It will let the girls enjoy themselves and have a celebration that allows them to relax."

Josh nodded his head, "I'll set up reservations. We can split everything like you said."

Stretching his large frame, Mark sighed, "Agreed, but do we tell them beforehand? I mean, ladies usually like to know these kinds of things."

Josh shook his head, "No, I think it should be a surprise until we pull up at the place. I don't think either one has been before and it will be a complete surprise to them both."

"It's a great idea, because the anniversary party's still two weeks away and it will give them a little break. But how will we get each of them to pack an overnight bag?" Mark swirled his cup of coffee, unsure of how to deal with a potentially delicate problem.

Josh frowned, "Yeah, that is a conundrum. Bales hates me to pack for her. The last time we went to Atlanta for a quick trip for work, I left half the things she said she had to have. Besides, going through my mom's stuff would be weird." He shivered but had no answer.

"We could just tell them to pack an overnight bag, but nothing else." Mark shrugged. "It would let them have an idea of how long we will be gone but nothing that really explains our plans."

Josh smirked, "That's be perfect. I can't tell you how many times growing up Mom was able to guess her presents. It was a family joke no one could surprise her, she's just too smart. We actually stopped asking her to guess, because it didn't matter what we got her, somehow she always knew."

"She's a very smart woman."

Nodding with a sly grin, Josh rubbed his hands. "Plus, having to be so secretive to keep my Mom from figuring out our plans will also drive Bales crazy. She loves surprises, but really hates waiting for them."

"Isn't a little early in the marriage to be driving Bailey crazy? Aren't you still supposed to be in the honeymoon phase of your marriage?"

Josh winked, "I've never enjoyed sparring with anyone more. Bailey and I actually enjoy the playful fun. I know for a fact when she drew up the dishwashing diagram, she was grinning the entire time she was using her colored pencils and markers."

"Oh, yes, the dishwasher diagram is legendary. Bales should market it. When I mentioned it to Kip and Becka, she wanted to know more details and when I said it was color-coded, she declared even Kip couldn't mess that up."

Josh laughed so loud the other coffee drinkers in the shop turned to stare a moment before returning to their coffee. "It's our special argument to show we love each other for our quirks, and I wouldn't want to spar with anyone else. Bales is my feisty redhead and I love her."

Mark laughed, "Well, I think that's everything then. Let me know if you need me to do anything else. I've got some writing I've got to do this morning and I know you're off to Atlanta for work."

"Will do. Oh, I know you have the Aston Martin. Do you want to drive all of us? It should be a pretty spring day by then."

"Sure. I can handle that. Just know it will be a tight squeeze for you and Bales in the backseat." Thinking of the crazy Georgia weather, Mark sent up a quick prayer it would be a nice day for a drive.

"That's fine. Mom keeps talking about how much she loves riding in it and I've been a little jealous."

"You're more than welcome to take it for a spin."

"I'll hold you to that. I mean, you are dating my mom. I should get some type of benefit from it, besides books autographed by the author."

The two men laughed and then went their separate ways. When Josh called later to say everything was set, Mark hoped he could hold his excitement for a week until it was time to reveal the special surprise.

Chapter Twenty-Three

"Ready, ladies?" Josh asked his mom and wife.

Bailey frowned at her husband. "Yes, but it would be nice to know where we're going."

"What part of surprise do you not understand?"

Hands on slim hips, Bailey fussed, "Joshua James Cabot! You've not told us anything but to dress up tonight and pack an overnight bag."

Kissing her instead of replying, Josh spread his arms wide, "Time to go."

Opening the front door to see Mark's convertible in the driveway with the top already down, he grabbed the luggage and led the two ladies out the door.

Mark held open the door for the women and Andrea kissed him on the cheek before sliding in. "Thank you."

"You're welcome." He closed their doors, before helping Josh put all of the luggage in the trunk. "Got everything?"

"I hope so. You wouldn't believe all the fussing they did because they didn't know what we were doing. You think we were planning a trip to the Arctic with all the questions they asked."

Chuckling, Mark said, "It's a woman thing, I think."

"Are you gentleman getting in?" Bailey gruffly called out.

Slamming the trunk shut, Josh winked at Mark, "My wife enjoys surprises but really hates waiting for them."

Mark glanced at Andrea sitting calmly in the front seat and was excited to treat his special lady. Starting the car, he cut the music down just a bit. "So, how many people are coming to your big anniversary party?"

"Well. We've gotten RSVPs from most everyone," Andrea shifted in her seat to glance at Bailey and Josh cuddled in the back.

"Yes," Bailey held Josh's hand. "We've got a lot of people who can make it and I talked to Michael this morning and his whole construction crew will be there. I've got our orders in for the food and hope to try out some new recipes this next week to have for the party."

"Are you sticking with the international theme?" Mark pulled out onto a back road and planned for a leisurely ride to their destination.

"She should be. I've been eating Thai, Chinese, Mexican, and even a few African dishes for the past week as she narrows down the meal plan."

Laughing, Andrea turned to Mark. "Be glad you canceled dinner plans on Tuesday. Bailey made something with goat and a green sauce that wasn't a big hit with Josh."

"It was awful. Too stringy for me. I think I can still taste it."

"You just don't have a sophisticated palate like Andrea and I," Bailey said.

Mark didn't miss the eye roll Andrea did, "Well, I had to meet with my editor unexpectedly. With me out of the state for this book, it's made things difficult."

"How did the meeting go?"

"Pretty well. I didn't realize how hard it would be to work over the phone to review my book. Seeing David's face as we discuss chapters gives me great insight into changes that need to be made."

"Have you thought about FaceTime or some video conferencing over the internet?" Bailey piped up from the back.

Mark looked in the rearview mirror back at the petite redhead. "That's genius. I can't believe I didn't think about it."

"That's how Grace and I chatted face-to-face when I was in Colorado Springs."

"I'll tell David and we'll set that up for next time."

"What do you mean... SNAILS?!?" Josh shifted away to look his wife in the eye, "Bailey Dawn Evans Cabot, are you trying to kill me?!?"

Mark and Andrea started to laugh as it sunk in for Josh, the dinner they had the other night was Bailey trying some culinary treats from France. As the young couple argued, Mark reached out to grab Andrea's hand. "I told Josh to tell you the place we're going is pet-friendly, but you didn't bring Muffin."

Andrea smiled. "Thank you for thinking of her, but Laura wanted to test out a dog for Brian now they're officially in Bailey's old house with a fenced in backyard."

"Yes, I remember her talking a few weeks ago about moving. It's good they're settled in."

"And not too soon. Her in-laws are moving down in June."

"Ahh!"

As Mark made a turn down another country back road, Andrea said, "I'm surprised you didn't know. Noah's spending the weekend with Laura and Brian. He was excited for the chance to prove to his parents he could take care of his own Neptune."

"That's probably why." Mark chuckled, reaching for her hand. "They're mad my girlfriend's going to be the reason they have to get a dog!"

He rubbed his thumb across her hand. "Any word from Jacob?"

"No," Andrea sighed, "But, I'm okay. I trust God to take care of my boy. Talking to you about it helped."

"I'm glad!"

"Are we there yet?"

Andrea and Mark looked up as Bailey asked again, "Are we there yet?"

Josh said, "Almost, Chef Bailey."

Bailey sent an eye roll his way. "Pluh-leease, my meal was so much better than the crazy computer show you dragged me to a few weeks ago. That's two hours of my life I won't get back."

"Children, please. We're about to turn on the road, and I told them two ADULT couples would be visiting." Mark smirked at them through the rearview mirror.

Andrea looked out the window and saw a beautiful driveway, stone and large rolling grassy fields spread out in a back-country road in Adairsville. "Oh, Mark. Really?" She turned to Josh, "You guys, didn't?"

Kissing a stunned Bailey, Josh laughingly said, "Surprise, Bailey, love of my life even if you are trying to kill me with your unique culinary cuisines."

Tears in her eyes, Bailey murmured just above a whisper, "I promise from now on, I'll give you fair warning and you can choose what you want to eat or not."

He looked into her watery green eyes. "It's probably best if you don't tell me everything you have me try. I trust you not to kill me and except for the goat, I've loved everything you've ever made."

Laughing, Bailey kissed him. "Deal, and no more goat."

Mark pulled up to a quaint guard shack. "Good afternoon. We're here for a one-year anniversary celebration."

"Congratulations!" An older gentleman grinned, leaning forward. "Have you been to Barnsley Gardens, before?"

"No," The ladies chimed in, the delight evident in their voices.

"Well," the gentleman winked, "You're in for a treat. The weather's perfect, the food's delightful, and there's always something fun to do on the grounds."

After giving Mark directions of where to check-in, the group followed the winding path toward the main grounds.

"I've wanted to visit since we moved to Cartersville, but never had a reason to come." Andrea was constantly moving her head back and forth to see the sights.

"I hear the food is amazing, along with the views."

Josh caught up in the girl's excitement nodded to Mark. "We wanted you two to have an anniversary celebration that didn't involve you doing all the planning, cooking, and organizing."

"Oh, Josh. You're such a good son."

"It was Josh's idea to do something."

"And Mark's idea to have it at Barnsley Gardens."

Parking, Mark turned to Andrea and said quietly, "It seemed elegant and classy, just like you, Andrea."

Touched all the way down to her toes, Andrea followed everyone into the lobby of the hotel and couldn't decide if she had ever been more surprised.

As the men checked them in, Andrea and Bailey walked around looking at all of the sights. Bailey whispered, "Did you know they were planning something like this?"

Andrea shook her head, "No clue."

"I actually feel bad for feeding Josh escargot now."

Falling against her daughter-in-law, Andrea's laughter filled the large open room.

"All set, girls. The staff's delivering our luggage." Mark took Andrea's hand. "I thought we could stroll out to our suites and see the sights as we go. We have dinner reservations at seven and should have time to settle into our rooms before dinner."

"Ready?" Josh put his arm around Bailey.

The two couples slowly walked the grounds, quietly following the staff who were carrying their things. When they finally arrived in front of a small cottage, Andrea exclaimed, "We're staying here?"

Holding the door open, Josh waved them in. "Yep. We're staying in a four-bedroom cottage on the grounds."

"Four-bedrooms?" Andrea frowned.

"Well, I didn't know if Bailey would still be speaking to me after I fussed about her meal the other day."

Bailey gently hit his arm. "Oh, you." She then flew into his arms, "You spoil me."

"It's one of my favorite parts of being married to you."

The couples walked into the cabin and as Andrea and Bailey marveled looking over every detail, Mark tipped the young man who carried their bags.

"Oh, Bailey, look at this clawfoot tub."

"Mom, did you see the mints on the pillows."

"Oh, wow, look at this view."

Mark and Josh stood in the living room, watching the ladies run back and forth, taking in all the details. Josh held out his fist and as Mark bumped it, as Josh said, "Totally nailed it!"

Mark watched Andrea's smiling face. "Definitely worth it."

After the ladies decided which rooms they wanted and unpacked, the two couples made their way to the Woodlands Grill Restaurant on the grounds. It was a bit of a walk from the cabin, but Andrea enjoyed holding Mark's hand along the way and seeing the smile on Josh and Bailey's faces.

She laid her head on Mark's broad shoulder, "This is so special, Honey. Thank you very much."

Mark kissed her hair. "I'm taking a page from Josh's book. I like spoiling you, too!"

Walking into the restaurant, Mark gave his name and time for their reservations. They were seated quickly and soon perused the menu.

"Oh, Mom. Look at this menu. I want to try everything."

Josh laughed, "I've seen you eat, you probably could."

"Now, kids," Mark laughed. "You'd just decided on a truce."

Andrea snorted, "You should have learned by now, their 'truce' usually lasts as long as it takes Josh to volunteer to load the dishwasher."

The couples were still laughing when their waiter came over to take their drink orders and list the specials. After he walked away, Mark took a sip of water. "How is the rest of the party planning going?"

Mouthwatering in anticipation of the appetizers on their way, Bailey unfolded her napkin. "Pretty well considering it's in twenty days."

Andrea nodded, "We're on schedule and Bailey almost has the whole menu ready."

"The only thing we have left to decide is what to do for party favors."

Turning to Mark, Andrea explained, "We want something that will advertise the business, but still fit into the theme."

Josh took a sip of water. "Well, you're a catering company and have been doing a lot of weddings lately... is there something you'd do for a wedding that would work for your business?"

Bailey and Andrea looked at each other thinking. Andrea moved to write in her notebook. "That's a good direction. We'll think about it." Turning to Josh, Andrea said, "Thank you, Sweetheart."

Cleaning his glasses, Josh said, "Well, it seemed fitting." He put them back on, "What do you even do at an anniversary party?"

Andrea said, "Well, we know we want to welcome everyone and dedicate the new spaces. I've got Pastor Graham set to pray over the buildings after we cut the ribbon."

"Then there's the food," Bailey blew a kiss at Josh. "Plus we're going to test out the dance floor."

He started to pull off his glasses again, but Bailey grabbed his hand. "It will be fine, Josh. We'll only dance to a slow one."

As Josh kissed his wife, their food arrived and talk soon revolved around the wonderful meal, before moving to more general topics. Andrea found herself struggling to remember when she had enjoyed an evening more. She loved seeing Mark interacting with Bailey and Josh like he was a part of the family.

After dessert, Mark leaned back. "That was amazing."

Bailey licked her fork one last time before adding, "No exaggeration. It was divine. I can't imagine how you guys could have topped tonight."

Josh winked at Mark and said to the ladies, "That's easy. Tomorrow you and Mom are having a spa day before we go home."

"Spa day?" The ladies cried out together.

Each kissed their guy, before Andrea asked, "What are you two going to do while we're relaxing?"

"Golfing," Josh swung an imaginary club.

"Golfing?" Andrea raised an eyebrow. "You don't golf, Josh."

"Mark's going to teach me."

Andrea looked at Mark who only shrugged and turned back to her son. "You do know golf is considered a sport, right?"

"Yes, but how hard can it be? It's just hitting a little ball around a big, open field."

Andrea laughed while she turned to Mark. "Please make sure you get some of his attempts on video."

Kissing her, Mark winked. "Will do!"

Helping her to rise, the group slowly started walking back to their cabins. It was late because they spent most of the evening talking over the wonderful meal. When they arrived back at the cabin, Mark tugged Andrea's arm. "Would you like to sit on the front porch with me a bit before we go in?"

She nodded, before settling down in his arms. After saying goodnight to Bailey and Josh, Andrea sighed with contentment. "This was wonderful, Mark."

"I'm glad you've enjoyed the evening." Glancing behind him at Bailey and Josh moving around the living room, he continued, "You've got some great kids. I've really enjoyed spending time with Bales and Josh. They're a fun couple."

"Yes, they keep me young."

Mark chuckled, "You keep me young."

Andrea felt a blush rising, and hoped in the moonlight it would be hard to see. She rested her head on his shoulder. "I've been blessed by each of them, and as a couple I couldn't love them more. They've never made me feel like a third wheel, even with them living in the big house, we've made it work."

"I was worried a bit how it would be spending time with them, but they're delightful and have embraced me with open arms."

"Well, they know you make me happy."

Kissing her, Mark sighed, "You make me happy, too!"

She settled back into his arms. "It's a good thing I love them so much. I'm a bit mad they won't be the first to marry in the new building."

Mark chuckled, his chest rising and falling against Andrea. "They would have had to wait a while."

"Yes, but it would have been nice to have more than two months to get them married. They tried to drive me crazy with that whirlwind wedding."

Rubbing his thumb across her hand, Mark asked, "Are you more upset they won't be the first ones married in the new building or how fast it happened for them?"

"You're right. I'm not really upset. It would just be nice to have the first wedding be family and not some strangers. I don't know the couple who will be married on June seventh. They just saw an advertisement and signed up."

"So, that's what's bothering you. You don't know the couple well and you feel it should be..."

"Someone I care about," Andrea was glad he understood. Sighing she continued, "It's silly, I know."

"No, it's not my love."

They sat in silence and as Andrea listened to the crickets singing in the woods, she told herself she was being silly.

"Andrea, my heart."

"Hmmm?"

"What if it was family that was married there first?"

Sitting up a bit to face him, Andrea could barely make out his face in the moonlight. "What do you mean?"

"Well, what if... well... blame it on Harold and Betty Lu, but well..."

"Mark?"

Mark sat up and moved to kneel in front of her. "Andrea Cora Cabot, would you marry me?"

"Mark?"

Neither spoke and Andrea found a thousand thoughts rushing through her head. *Is he crazy? Am I crazy to be considering it?!? I do love him, and as he said, Harold and Betty had the right idea, we're not getting any younger.*

"Andrea? Are you okay? You're awful quiet. Do you think I've lost my mind?"

"No, because I might have lost mine, too!"

"Do you love me?"

Tears in her eyes, she nodded. "I really do!"

"Do you think a second marriage would be out of the question for us?"

"No."

"Do you think May twenty-ninth is too soon?"

Andrea didn't speak but wondered at his words.

Mark cleared his throat, "I do want to marry you, Andrea. I'll wait longer if you want because this is out of the blue... but you should know I want to marry you no matter how long you make me wait."

Tears in her eyes, Andrea found it hard to speak. She leaned forward and kissed him. *Lord, are we being crazy?*

Feeling at peace, Andrea wrapped her arms around Mark. "Let's do this. Let's get married in only twenty days."

Mark leaned back and she could see the shock on his face even in the dim light. "We're nuts."

Laughing, Andrea agreed. "We are, but I love we're being crazy together."

"Should we go tell Josh and Bales?"

"No, I think I have a better idea."

Kissing, it was a while before they started making plans.

Chapter Twenty-Four

"I must have been out of my mind to let Andrea talk me into this."

Maggie looked up from packing the bag she was packing. "If I remember right, this was your idea."

"No, this was definitely her idea." Mark paused in stuffing his shaving kit into his suitcase.

Maggie started laughing so hard she had to set down the bag she was helping to pack. "Mark Lawson Hastings! You called me over two weeks ago and said you came up with a brilliant idea and you two needed my help."

Mark straighten his tie. "Oh, yeah. I did say that, didn't I."

"Now, you sound like Kip did growing up when he finally admitted a mistake."

"Hush, woman. You're not helping. I know marrying Andrea isn't a mistake, I just not sure how I feel about surprising everyone. Josh might kill me on the spot."

"It will be fine. It's just nerves." Maggie walked over to fix his tie. "You and Andrea are perfect for each other and I couldn't be happier. I'm sure Josh will feel the same way."

"I hope so. I don't know how I'd feel if my mother planned a secret ceremony to marry some strange guy."

"You're not some strange guy. You're Mark Lawson Hastings, author, father of Kip, grandfather of Noah and Eva…"

"And terrified fiancé of Andrea Cabot…"

"It will be fine." Winking at him, Maggie asked, "All set?"

"I think so, or at least as ready as I will be. This has been the longest day of my life. The party should've been planned for in the morning, not seven at night."

"Well, I've got Andrea's things and the flowers for her bouquet."

Mark stilled Maggie's hands. "Thanks for doing this, Mags. We couldn't have pulled off this surprise wedding without you. I thought Andrea was crazy to mention you helping, but she was right, as always."

"I think it's wonderful and I'm honored you chose me to help." Tears in her eyes, Maggie hugged him. "I told Andrea I wanted us to be friends and I'm glad she knew I meant it."

"Well, she wanted you and your family here for the wedding and knew we'd have to tell you to get you here all the way from Chicago on the spur of the moment."

"Wise woman, you're marrying."

"Don't I know it."

"Good." She walked over to grab the bag Andrea would be taking on their quick honeymoon weekend. "Now, let's go get you two married."

Mark paled just a bit, but helped his ex-wife to the car, grateful she was the special woman she was. *It's not every ex-wife who would help her former husband and his girlfriend pull off a surprise, secret wedding in front of a huge room full of people.*

"Mom, are you okay? You're awful nervous for an anniversary party. That's the third thing you've dropped this morning."

Andrea looked up from the last gift bag she was tying, hoping she didn't look as nervous as she felt. "It's okay, Josh. Just ready to get the party started. I know everyone will be arriving soon and well… I'm not fond of waiting."

They have no idea. I was hoping they wouldn't see me adding the wedding favors, Mark and I had created at the last minute to celebrate our special day. Putting the last roll of mints with their initials and the words 'Mint for each other' in the bags, she sighed. *Bales and I decided the gift bags should showcase wedding and party favors we can offer for the business but I wanted to add something specifically for my wedding to Mark. The print shop didn't get them done until late last night and this was the first chance, I had to add them.* Hiding a smile, she thought, *not that anyone will need favors to remember this surprise wedding Mark and I have planned.*

Bailey came rushing into the kitchen, "Everyone's starting to arrive. I saw Mags and Mark pull up with the rest of the Hasting's crew right behind them. I didn't know the Miller family would be coming. That's sweet. Were they already planning on coming down for the end of the school?"

Andrea didn't reply but rushed out to the hall mirror to check her makeup before she went to track down Mark and Mags. *I'm glad I took a page out of Betty's wedding plans and picked a simple blue dress for today. It's silly to wear white at my age.*

She smoothed a few imaginary wrinkles in her dress before she ran her hand through her hair and then turned to go find her fiancé and his ex-wife. She had taken her luggage for the honeymoon to Maggie yesterday to put in Mark's car. She was afraid if Bailey saw packed bags, she would get suspicious.

Waving to people as they arrived, she spied Mark's Aston Martin parked near the cottage entrance. Before she could get close to Mark, Maggie grabbed her in a big hug.

"Andrea, I'm so happy for you two." Whispering, Maggie continued, "You both have made me very happy and I'm so glad you let me in on the big secret."

"Well, only you and Pastor Graham know."

"I'm honored." Turning to Mark, Mags put her hands on her hips. "So, what's the plan?"

"We've talked with Pastor Winston and after Bailey and I welcome everyone and thank them for coming, she and I will cut the ribbon and then Pastor will pray."

Mark came up and put his arm around Andrea. "Then we get married and party for the rest of the night. I'm planning to dance most of the night with my bride."

"Love it!" Maggie's smile practically lit up the evening sky. *Lord, they are too cute. I'm so glad to have a part in getting them together.*

"Yes, if you can bring the bouquet to me after Pastor Winston prays, we'll start the ceremony."

"I'm going to have Kip stand up and be my best man after I ask him…"

Andrea continued, "And I'll ask Bales to be my Matron of Honor."

"We both wanted simple, easy, and..." Mark winked at his fiancée, "Faster than Bales wedding because my Andrea, as it turns out, is competitive."

The three of them laughed before Andrea showed Maggie where she could hide the bouquet until it was time, just missing Bailey coming around the corner. When Bailey offered to give Maggie a tour of the building, Andreas was glad because it gave her time to calm her nerves.

"Andrea?"

"Yes," Andrea turned, her dress swishing in the light breeze to see Mark standing close holding out a small box.

"I wanted you to have this before the wedding." He stepped closer, he words soft.

Taking the small ring box, Andrea saw a beautiful diamond ring, surrounded by blue topaz. "It's my birthstone!"

Mark took the ring from her and put it gently on her finger. "I thought my December born wife deserved an engagement ring that reminded her how special I think her birthday is, because without December twenty-third, I wouldn't have my Andrea Cabot, soon to be, Hastings."

"Oh, Mark! It's beautiful." She held her hand out to look at it shining before holding his cheek for a kiss. "Thank you! I know we talked about not getting an engagement ring until later because we're surprising everyone with the wedding..." Tears in her soft, brown eyes, Andrea paused, "But, I didn't feel right not getting married without something on my hand. You're very thoughtful."

"Soon, my dear, we will be married and you can show this ring off to the whole world."

Andrea stared at her ring off and on as they walked arm in arm into the new reception building. *Soon, Lord, soon I'll be Mrs. Hastings, and I can't wait!*

"Hi, Noah. Are you having fun?"

"Yes, Mrs. Andrea. Brian and I have been playing with Muffin. Mom and Dad said next weekend when school's out, we're going to get a dog."

"That's wonderful, Noah. I know how much you've been wanting one."

"I told my dad it was unfair Kip Saturn's son didn't have his own Neptune."

Andrea laughed, hugging the little boy. *Thank You, Lord, for bringing Noah into my life. He's been more than a blessing, also a good friend. Very shortly, I'll be his other grandmother and I couldn't be happier about it. I hope Noah will be excited about it, too!*

"Mom, the pastor's looking for you. He said it's time to start."

She took a deep breath, "Thanks, Josh." She moved to hug him, holding onto his sleeve a moment. "Stay close, I'll need you soon." *He doesn't know it, but he will be the one walking me down the aisle.*

"Andrea, there you are. Pastor Winston's ready to say the blessing and we need to formally welcome everyone." Bailey's face was flushed with excitement and Andrea had a feeling hers was a bit red from nerves of her own.

Taking a deep breath, Andrea called out to the large crowd, "Welcome everyone to the Taste & See Catering's one-year anniversary and dedication celebration."

Everyone cheered and as Andrea looked out over their friends and families' faces, she smiled at Josh before winking at Mark.

"Thank you all for coming to celebrate with Bailey and I. We wouldn't be here if it wasn't for all of your support, love, and encouragement."

Bailey stepped up next to Andrea. "We've asked Pastor Graham Winston to pray a special prayer and blessings over the new buildings and for all of the future couples who will be celebrating in this space."

Putting her arm around Andrea, Bailey continued, "This little plot of land will always hold a special place in my heart... it's where I found my family, my God, and my purpose. Thank you, everyone, for being here to celebrate with us."

The two ladies walked over to cut the ribbon at the front of the large banquet hall space where Michael had built a grand fireplace. As Bailey and Andrea held onto the large scissors, a shout went up when the ribbon fell to the floor.

Pastor Graham walked to the center of the aisle and said in a deep, booming voice, "Let's bow our heads."

As people closed their eyes, Mark moved closer to Andrea when the pastor started his prayer.

"Thank You, Lord, for this special day to celebrate Your blessings on Taste & See Catering. These ladies have worked long and hard to make this business a godly endeavor which honors You. Please bless their efforts and the families who will celebrate their special events in this location, everything from birthday parties to weddings. May each bride and groom married on this property be blessed while growing closer to each other and to You. And may the first wedding on this property be extra special as Mark Hastings and Andrea Cabot say their vows in just a few moments. Amen."

Everyone had been very hushed during the prayer, but after Pastor Graham's words, whispers quickly grew to shouted questions echoing through the large space.

When Andrea and Mark raised their heads, everyone was staring at them with shocked looks on their faces. Mark cleared his throat, "Andrea and I decided it was only right the first wedding at Taste & See's new facility be in the family."

Taking Mark's arm, Andrea grinned. "Plus, I couldn't let Bailey have the fastest wedding in the family."

Bailey and Josh ran up to grab Andrea. "Mom, I can't believe this."

"This is crazy… and wonderful," Bailey had tears in her eyes.

"I'm glad you think so because I want you to be my Matron of Honor."

Bailey couldn't speak but only nodded tears falling down her face.

Kip and his family walked up, Noah jumping up and down. "You're going to be my Grandmother now, Ms. Andrea."

Andrea bent down to Noah. "Yes, I thought you'd be excited since I think you were hoping for this all along."

Noah blushed, "Of course! Why do you think I kept trying to have you meet my grandpa all the time?"

Mark looked down at his grandson and winked, "Good job, young man."

"Thanks, Grandpa. I knew Mrs. Andrea was perfect for you."

Kip put his hand on his son's head, ruffling his hair. "Chip off the old block."

Mark put his arm on Kip's shoulder. "I'd be honored if you'd be my best man."

"I'd love to, Dad."

"Josh, would you walk me down the aisle?" Andrea looked up at him with tears in her brown eyes.

Josh came up to kiss his mother's cheek. "I wouldn't have it any other way."

Everyone quickly moved to get in their places. Guests settled down in the chairs and as Bailey, Josh, and Andrea stood in the back, Bailey stopped and then slapped her forehead. "That's why you INSISTED the chairs be set up like a wedding. It wasn't to show people how it could look, but be set up for YOUR wedding!"

"You're a very sneaky woman," Josh kissed his mother's cheek.

"Thank you, Son."

"Here you are, Andrea. One bouquet of flowers, plus your something borrowed, new, and blue."

Andrea smiled at Maggie. "Thank you, Mags."

Bailey looked at the bouquet. "What's your borrowed, new, and blue?"

Holding the blue flowers, Andrea looked down at her dress. "For the blue, I have my dress, plus the orchids and for the old, I have the earrings James gave me, and for something borrowed, Maggie lent me a necklace, and for the something new..."

Maggie smiled as she chimed in, "Our friendship."

Bailey hugged her mother-in-law. "Perfect." Before she could continue, the music started, "That's my cue."

As she walked down the aisle, Josh moved closer to his mom and took her arm. "I'm very happy for you, Mom. I think Mark's a great guy and will be good for you."

Heart swelling, Andrea squeezed his arm. "Thank you, sweetie. You've grown into a wonderful young man. I can't tell you how happy I am you're okay with all of this."

"Well, a bit more of a warning would have been nice, but this is perfect for you."

"Thank you for understanding. We wanted something simple and quiet since this is technically a second wedding for both us."

The wedding march began and Josh escorted his mother down the aisle. When he placed her hands in Mark's, he nodded at the older man, confident he was putting his mother in good hands.

Pastor Graham started the simple ceremony, and before she knew it, she was saying "I do" to Mark Lawson Hastings.

"You may now kiss the bride."

With a twinkle in his eye, Mark leaned forward to take Andrea in his arms. Kissing her soundly he leaned back to the shouts and cheers, "Nice to meet you, Mrs. Andrea Hastings."

Andrea laughed, kissing him a second time. "Nice to meet you, Mr. Hastings."

They turned to face the crowd of cheering friends and family as Pastor Graham announced, "I proudly present to you, Mr. and Mrs. Mark Hastings."

Marching down the aisle arm in arm, Andrea looked out at the evening sky and smiled up to Heaven. *Thank You, Lord, for not listening to this old woman's idea about what her life should like, but renewing my purpose and love by bringing this man into my life.*

The End

Dear Reader,

Thank you for reading my fourth novel in the Grace Series. A new year means new books and I'm excited to be working on new stories featuring characters mentioned in my previous novels.

This current novel featured Andrea Cabot, a widow who learned she wasn't as set in her ways as she thought when it came to love. I enjoyed writing this story and the funny misunderstanding about Andrea's age. It was wonderful to see more of Josh and Bailey's relationship, and quite a few weddings were thrown in of new and old friends.

I'm busy writing more stories in the Grace Series. My next novel, Healing Grace, the fifth novel in the Grace Series will feature Laura Flowers and Jacob Cabot, Andrea's youngest son, a Marine. There are two chapters for this new novel at the end of this book giving you a glimpse of the novel coming out in August 2019.

The sixth novel, Giving Grace will feature Sharon Pruitt and Preston Dyson, III, both in the restaurant business. I'm excited about this novel because it will feature someone with Celiac disease, a recent diagnosis in my own life. This novel will have a lot of true Southern style.

The seventh novel in the Grace Series is Saving Grace featuring Ivy Ingles and Tony Jett who both learn about God's saving grace when an unexpected blessing comes their way.

Be sure to check out my website for more details and sign up for the blog on my website to get sneak peeks.

I love to hear from my readers and would enjoy getting to know you better. Please feel free to reach out to me!

   www.acboulier.com
   www.facebook.com/acboulier
   www.twitter.com/acboulier
   www.instagram.com/acboulier_author
   www.pinterest.com/acboulier

Until next time, may God's grace surround you,

Coming August 2019

Healing Grace

Book Five in the Grace Series

If Time Doesn't Heal Wounds, Will God?

Laura Flowers has sworn off men after an abusive marriage which finally ended when her husband was killed in action while in the army. Her only goal now is to raise her son, Brian, to be a loving, Christian man and not turn into a rebellious kid under her in-laws' influence. A battle which she seemed to be losing.

Jacob Cabot, Andrea's youngest son in the Marines has been discharged from the military because of physical injuries and even more mental scars. Lost and unsure who he is now he's not an active Marine, Jacob must find a new place in this civilian world. Under his mother's influence, Jacob joins the mentoring program at a local elementary school and he becomes a mentor to Brian Flowers.

Can these three hurting people learn about God's
Healing Grace to find their way back home?

AVAILABLE AUGUST 30, 2019

Prologue

April 2014

"I've decided to retire after this mission."

Jacob looked over at Tyler, and snorted, "Yeah, right. You know we're lifers. In basic training, we both said they'd bury us in our uniforms."

"I'm not kidding, Jacob. This is my last mission. I've filled out the paperwork and everything. It's set in stone."

Adjusting the scope on his rifle, Jacob turned slightly toward Tyler to see if he was joking or not. Seeing the clear brown eyes staring at him without blinking, Jacob felt a stone drop in his stomach. "Why? We've always talked about being soldiers until we're old and gray, and while you're old, you're not gray."

Glancing at his watch, Jacob thought, *I hope this truck shows up soon. We've been here since one in the morning and I'm ready to grab some shut eye.*

"I'm barely two years older than you. Besides, you're one to talk, I've seen you hiding those gray hairs with shorter and shorter haircuts."

"Hey, I'm still only twenty-six." Jacob turned back to watch the road, waiting for the truck to arrive.

"I want to meet someone and start a family before I'm too old to play with my kids."

"Where's this coming from?"

Tyler shifted slightly, his movements were barely noticeable, since the two men were waiting for their target to arrive. Sweat trickled down Tyler's nose, but he was trained to ignore everything and keep movements to a minimum when they were out on a dangerous mission where the slightest move could get you and your brothers killed.

Holding the binoculars, he scanned the area before he sighed, "I've been thinking about this for a while, but when Tank died a few months ago, well..."

"That was an accident. It wasn't even in combat."

"I know that's what really got me thinking. Our time on earth is only for a short moment in the grand scheme of things and I really want what time I have left on this earth to count for something. Raise another generation, continue the family line kind of thing."

Seeing movement, Jacob paused to reply but saw it was only a small animal in the distance looking for food. "This is awful deep thinking for a jarhead."

"Just because you have the intellect of a spoon..." Tyler checked their rear, before continuing, "I'm thinking I want to own a restaurant or coffee shop, maybe a Chick-fil-A or something."

"I've seen you cook."

"I'll hire people."

Jacob turned ever so slightly to stare at Tyler, his eyes wide. "You're really serious."

"Umm... yeah, dummy. That's what I've been trying to tell you."

"And you thought on a mission where we're to takeout a big shot bad guy was a good time to tell me?!?"

Sighing, Tyler said quietly, "I've been trying to tell you for weeks, but I haven't gotten up the nerve. I know this wasn't our plan."

"No..."

"What was that?"

Jacob looked over the ridge they were hiding on and saw a dust cloud rising in the distance. "I think this is them."

The two men settled into their positions and years of training took over. Jacob always felt the few minutes before he pulled the trigger were the longest moments of his life. Being trained as a sniper had made his dad so proud, but lately Jacob was becoming haunted by the eyes of the men he'd killed. *Maybe Tyler has the right idea, I know what I'm doing is important, but I never expected it to be this hard. I might not be as tough as my dad thought.*

Noise from the truck became almost deafening as Jacob saw more than one in a long line of vehicles. *Our intel didn't say there would be more than one truck.*

Looking through his scope for the target, Jacob took a deep breath as Tyler counted out, "One, Two, Three."

On the count of three, Jacob took a shot that normally would have made someone's career. He knew he'd hit his mark when the first truck veered off the road. Before he could see what was going on, he and Tyler grabbed what little gear they brought and made their exit.

"Move," Tyler barked. He didn't even wait, but broke out into a dead run. "We're going to have company soon."

Jacob didn't reply, already running down the steep incline of the ridge they had staked out. All thoughts ceased as he concentrated on his breathing. He heard Tyler right behind him. Not hearing any signs of pursuit, Jacob smiled. *We're going to make it.*

BOOM. BOOM.

Before Jacob finished his thought, he was flying through the air, dust and dirt in a thick blanket. *Grenade. No wondering they weren't pursuing us*, he thought seconds before he passed out.

What seemed like hours later, Jacob grabbed his head, unable to stop the ringing in his ears. *What a headache! Where am I?* "TYLER!"

Jacob jerked up and saw the world spin. Worried he was going to toss the protein bar he had earlier, he moved slowly looking for Tyler. The ringing in his head made it hard to concentrate but over to his left, he saw the crumpled form of Tyler Clark. Rushing over to his friend, Jacob checked for a pulse and nearly sobbed with relief when he found one.

"Come on Ty. Wake up and insult me."

Turning Tyler over, Jacob started checking his injuries and was worried to see he had a deep head wound. Ripping his own uniform, Jacob worked to stop the bleeding.

"Ouch, Jacob. That hurts. Stop it."

"You're bleeding, you big idiot."

"Yeah, well, you're making it worse."

"You must have a terrible head injury if that's all you can come up with."

"Give me a moment. I did just get hit with a grenade."

"Big baby, so did I."

"Yeah, well, I was closer." Coughing blood, Tyler wiped his mouth but made no other movement.

Jacob groaned, but held it in, because it made his head throb. "Big baby." *This is bad, Lord.* "We need to get out of here."

"Jacob, I can't walk."

"I know, I'm going to carry you."

Coughing more blood, Tyler growled, "No, you need to get out of here."

"No man left behind."

"I'm a dead man."

"Bite your tongue."

"I think I did when I landed."

"See, a sense of humor, you're going to be okay."

Tyler cut his eyes at Jacob but said nothing. He could see his friend was in no better shape than he was with blood pouring down his own head and shrapnel in his leg, neither paying attention to the multiple cuts and bruises covering them both.

"Go, Jacob. I think I've got a punctured lung among other things."

"You're no doctor..."

"Jacob, I outrank you, and I'm telling you to get out of here. That's an order."

"Shut up. You're injured so I'm declaring you unfit for command and I'm taking over."

"Bull...."

"Now, now. What would your mother say?"

Before Tyler could reply, Jacob hoisted him onto his back in a fireman's carry and prayed this wouldn't instantly kill him with a punctured lung. "We've got to get moving Tyler, so hush and concentrate on not dying."

"Ha ha. You're a regular comedian."

Jacob didn't reply but focused on moving as quickly as possible without throwing up. His head swam and the burning in his hip was almost unbearable, but he knew of the two, he was in better shape.

Walking quickly, he made good time and kept telling Tyler it was going to be okay. It looked like the insurgents just tossed a few grenades and then made a run for it, which suited Jacob just fine. *They won't be far behind. They'll get reinforcements and will soon be crawling all over the place. I know I hit our target, so it will take them a bit to regroup.*

Jacob walked for hours before he found a small cave and decided to take a break and give Tyler some water if he could stand it. Carefully laying his friend down, Jacob worried when Tyler didn't open his eyes. The trip had been rough for his friend. Moans proceed by gasps of air had been the only sign he was still hanging on.

"Come on, Ty." Pulling out some water, Jacob held the canteen to his lips. "Drink just a sip and then we'll get going."

Tyler's eyes fluttered open. "Jacob. You need to leave me."

"Not going to happen."

Coughing blood, Tyler sighed, "I always knew... that's why I wanted out..."

"What are you mumbling about..." Jacob was worried Tyler was fighting a fever and was delirious by his rambling.

Tyler looked up at Jacob, his eyes red, but clear, before he strangled out, "I always knew you were meant for something special. The way you escaped death, over and over, I knew God had to have a special plan for your life."

"What are you mumbling about? You're crazy!"

Moving to sit up, Tyler groaned, "No, I'm not. You've escaped death three times now." Coughing blood, he spat out, "THREE! Each time, you should've died, but you didn't. I KNOW God has a plan for you, Jacob. You need to stop running from it."

Jacob shook his head at his friend. *It's the fever. He's never been religious before. We both grew up in church, but we've always joked how religion isn't good for soldiers.*

"I want you to know, I've made my peace with God and I'm going to be okay. But, you need to do the same."

"TY..."

"It's okay, Jacob. You're my best friend and always will be. Just promise me you'll figure out what God has planned for you."

"TY, I can't..."

"Promise!" Tyler grabbed Jacob's hand, squeezing hard. "Promise me. A Marine's promise."

"I promise," Jacob could feel tears falling down his suntanned cheeks. "But I'm getting you back to base. Just hold on. Then we'll get out together."

Tyler whispered, "Don't forget your promise."

Jacob picked up his friend, determined to get him back to camp and to a doctor. He kept saying over and over, "Hold on Tyler. That's an order. Hold on."

After what seemed like days, Jacob saw the base only a mile away. "Thank God," he said, before calling to Tyler over his shoulder. "We're here Ty. You're going to be okay."

Unable to move another step, Jacob shot Tyler's pistol and then collapsed on the ground. *The perimeter guards will find us and get us help. Just hold on a bit longer, Ty.*

Jacob blacked out, but not before he glimpsed boots running his way. After that, he was constantly in and out of consciousness, hearing only bits and pieces of conversation.

"... he's bleeding out... let's get him to the infirmary... that hip is bad... he'll need surgery... I don't know if we can save the leg or not... clear the way... stat..."

Just before he was taken into surgery and put under, Jacob heard one of the doctors say to a nurse prepping him, "... Clark's dead, we can't do anything for him... it's a miracle Cabot made it back... it was a seven-mile walk on that bad hip... I don't know if we can save the leg..."

Then the anesthesia kicked in and Jacob drifted off to sleep.

Chapter One

July 2014

Feet hitting the ground, a small dust cloud rose up, the only movement in the still night. "Thank you, Sir, for the ride. I really appreciate it."

"No, thank you for your service, Soldier. I'm always happy to give a serviceman a ride." The trucker looked out at the empty field and asked again, "Are you sure there's a house around here? I don't see any lights at all."

A smile brightened his tan face as Jacob chuckled. "Yes, sir. It's just down the road, but I'll walk. I don't want to wake the family."

Putting the truck in gear, the old trucker waved, "Well then, welcome home, Soldier."

Jacob watched the truck drive off, the noise of the rig echoing in the quiet little town his mother moved to after his dad died. Picking up his duffle bag, he turned his feet toward his new home and only winced a bit at the pain in his hip. He remembered what the doctors said about taking it easy, not sitting or standing too long without moving or the pain would be worse. A two-hour truck ride late at night fell into the too long category.

"Yeah, right. I'm a soldier. Like pain will stop me," he muttered to the crickets chippering.

Making a slow, steady walk toward the big house his mother owned, Jacob was grateful the trucker picked him up shortly after he left the airport. *It would have been a longer walk than I would've liked from the Atlanta airport to the suburbs of Cartersville.*

Ignoring his limp, he rounded the corner of the long driveway and sighed to see his mother's place. *Home, at least for a while.*

Too tired to even talk to himself, he made his way around to the back of the house. He hoped his brother Joshua would be awake. *He was always a night owl.* Jacob didn't want to sleep out on the porch, but would if no one was up. *I've slept in much worse places and it isn't even raining.*

Not seeing lights, he turned around. *Porch, it is.* Disappointed Joshua was asleep, Jacob thought, *it is after one a.m. I'm sure Joshua has work in the morning.* He lifted his t-shirt off his skin a moment, and muttered, "I thought one good thing about being home would mean it wouldn't be so stinking hot. I know it's July, but it's north Georgia, not Afghanistan.

Walking around front, Jacob paused to see a light on in the kitchen. He started to reach for his gun, and remembered it was packed in his duffle bag. Reminding himself he was in Georgia and not surrounded by terrorists, he realized it was his mother getting a midnight snack and not someone out to kill him.

"I'll surprise her. I haven't seen Mom in over a year," Jacob muttered. He checked the back-kitchen door and wasn't surprised to find it was unlocked. *Civilians.*

Gently opening it, Jacob lightly stepped inside to his mother's catering kitchen and mentally agreed with Joshua this place was too big for his widowed mother to be rumbling around in. He carefully lowered his bag down by the pantry and moved closer to the largest refrigerator he had ever seen in a residential kitchen.

Not making a sound, he could see his mother in a red robe, head down as she was rifling through the fridge. Hearing her mutter about men moving things around, he paused. *She sounds different. Can you get a cold in a miserably hot July?*

Jacob moved quickly and wrapped his Mom in a big bear hug. "Hi, Mom! Guess who's home."

"AAHHH!"

The scream coming from his petite mother was deafening. "Ouch, stop hitting me." Jacob backed up, ducking food and plastic containers thrown at him with a surprisingly strong right arm. "Stop, Mom. It's me."

"Who are you? You don't belong here. AND I'M NOT YOUR MOTHER!"

Before Jacob could say another word, the lights flashed on, and he was nearly blinded. He heard someone roar, "What's going on? Bailey are you okay?"

"There's some strange guy in here calling me mother! Where's Muffin when you need her? She needs to bite him or something."

Jacob opened his eyes to see a petite redhead holding the largest butcher knife he had ever seen. "Hey, hold on..." Backing up, Jacob waved his hands in surrender. "I must have the wrong place..." *She moved awful fast to get that knife. I'm not that slow, am I?*

"Jacob?"

Turning, Jacob looked at the man in boxers standing in the doorway with a large bat in his hands. Shocked, he fell to the ground, "Joshua?"

Joshua put down the bat and a large grin stretched across his face. "Hey, what are you doing here? When did you get in?"

"Jacob?" Bailey looked over at the tan, muscled man and saw some very familiar green eyes looking back at her. Putting down the butcher knife, Bailey sighed, *Lord, am I ever going to meet someone in Andrea's family not involving some type of lethal weapon?!?*

Joshua came forward to help his brother to his feet and grabbed him in a big hug. "I'm so glad you're here." Looking over at his wife, he chuckled, "And in one piece! What were you thinking?"

Jacob looked at the petite redhead with hair sticking up and shrugged. "She caught me by surprise."

Joshua roared with laughter. "It's Bailey's curse, taking out the Cabot men. At least your clothes are intact. I never did save that suit."

Jacob looked at Joshua and then Bailey in her nightgown. "Man, is Mom here? Does she know about you playing house with the redhead?"

Bailey crossed her arms, and smirked, "She should, this was her idea!"

"What?" Jacob's mouth fell open, *Mom's okay with Joshua's girlfriend sleeping over?!? Maybe I was more injured than I thought.*

Still laughing, Joshua pointed, "Jacob, meet my wife, Bailey."

"Wife!" Whipping his head from Joshua and then back to Bailey, he felt his knees go weak. "Wife? When did you get married?"

"December!" The married couple said in unison.

Jacob collapsed in a chair at the kitchen table and looked at his older brother. "Married? You were married over six months ago?!?"

Bailey walked over to stand in front of Jacob and extended her hand. "Hi, I'm Bailey. Your sister-in-law."

"And co-owner of Taste & See Catering with Mom." Joshua winked at his favorite redhead.

Putting out his hand, Jacob shook the petite woman's hand and marveled. "When it isn't so late, you'll have to tell me how that happened. Joshua was never one to get the pretty ladies."

Bailey blushed, and Joshua put his arm around his wife. "Get your own, brother. I don't share."

Jacob snorted. "No thanks. I'm good." Looking down at his hands, he muttered, "I guess I missed more than I thought being gone for over a year."

"You have no idea." Joshua looked at his younger brother. *He looks older than me, so tired, worn, and weary. I have no idea what he's gone through serving our country, but it's made his hair start to go white.*

Putting his arm on Jacob's shoulder, he didn't miss the slight panic in his brother's eyes. "Mom and I sent you emails every week to let you know everything going on."

Nodding, Jacob sighed, "Yeah. I'm sure. I just didn't have much access to the internet where I was and once, I realized I was coming home, I decided to wait and just catch up when I got here."

He smirked at his slightly bigger family and let out a low chuckle. "Guess I should've read my email first."

"You could say that! There are quite a few surprises for you."

A large yawn stopped his reply for a moment. "I'm realizing that, but I'm sure everything else can wait until the morning."

Bailey and Joshua both noticed the dark circles under his eyes and when Bailey gave her husband a look, Joshua said, "You need sleep, baby brother. The guest room downstairs is ready for you tonight."

"Thanks. I'm too tired to argue." Starting to stand up, Jacob made his way over to the pantry to grab his things. Slinging it over his shoulder, he raised an eyebrow, "I'm surprised Mom isn't down here. She wasn't a heavy sleeper."

"She's not here." Bailey moved Jacob's chair back under the table.

"Yeah, she's on her honeymoon."

"HONEYMOON?!?" Dropping his bag with a loud clunk, Jacob's face lost all color. "You weren't kidding about missing out on a lot of surprises."

"Yeah, well wait until you meet Mark." Joshua's grin was evil as he winked at Bailey and began picking up the items his wife had thrown at his brother. "They were married at the end of May but were only able to get away for a long honeymoon this week with all of the weddings and events the catering business had scheduled in June."

"It's been busy, but Mark really wanted to take her Ireland, since she's always wanted to go. They'll be back in a few days."

Picking up his bag again, Jacob looked at Joshua and gave him a hard look. "Is he good enough for her?"

"Yes, Jacob. They're good together. You'll see."

"I promise, brother-in-law, Mark and Andrea are perfect for each other."

"Well, we'll see." Yawning again, Jacob paused in the doorway, "Anything else I need to know?"

Joshua shook his head no. "Nope, that's it for big surprises. You've had enough for one night."

"That's the truth. I'll see you both in the morning."

Jacob started walking back toward the guest room when he turned and looked at Bailey, "Welcome to the family, Bailey. You seem to be good for Josh. I've never seen him look happier."

Before Bailey could reply, Jacob had left for bed and the kitchen was silent, except for Joshua putting up the last of the thrown food. "Sorry about the mess, Honey."

"It's okay, B. I'm just glad it wasn't a burglar."

Bailey chuckled, "I think I did pretty good with what I had."

Joshua put his arms around his wife and grinned. "You defended yourself very well and Jacob's clothing is intact. You're improving."

She slapped his hand away, "Oh you!" Pushing hair out of her eyes, she stuck out her tongue. "You're going to have to let the ruined suit go... I mean, you did get me out of the deal."

"That's true."

They made their way upstairs talking quietly. Joshua opened the bedroom door. "Why were you up anyway? You're usually a sound sleeper."

"I was hungry?"

"Did you get anything to eat before you attacked Jacob?"

Bailey threw her robe at him, "I'm not hungry anymore."

Joshua raised an eyebrow but tossed the robe aside as he climbed in bed. "You've been acting very strange lately."

"Hmmm..." Bailey didn't reply but crawled into bed beside her husband. "Why didn't you tell Jacob who Mark actually is?"

Gathering his wife into his arms, Joshua couldn't hide a devilish grin. "Well... That's one surprise for tomorrow. We couldn't make him suffer anymore tonight."

"Hmmm... You just wanted to make sure he was awake for the surprise about your new stepdad being Mark Lawson, author of the kid series you both love."

Chuckling, Joshua wiggled his eyebrows, "Maybe."

"Well, then I think now is the perfect time for your own surprise."

"Huh?" Joshua sat up a little to look at Bailey smirking in the dim light from her nightstand. "What surprise?"

"Josh, I'm pregnant!"

"PREGNANT?!?"

"Shush, you'll wake poor Jacob and he looks like he needs to sleep a week."

"Pregnant, as in having a baby?"

"Yes, sweetie, as in we're having a baby in March, by the way."

Joshua didn't speak but stared at his wife in shock.

"Josh, honey, are you breathing?" Bailey started to panic. *We didn't talk about having kids this soon, but I thought...*

Before she finished the thought, Joshua grabbed her in a big hug. "A baby, we're having a baby!"

"So… you're happy?"

"Of course, I'm happy! We're having a baby!"

Sighing with relief, Bailey poked him. "You had me worried for a minute."

"Well, the Cabot men have trouble with big news. It takes a while to sink in."

Reaching to turn off the light, she turned quickly back toward Joshua when he groaned, "Oh, no!"

"What, I thought you were happy?!?"

"I am, but Aiden!"

"What about Aiden? He and Carrie will be thrilled."

Shaking his head, Joshua's eyes were wide with fear. "So, I umm… I kind of played some pranks on Aiden when I found out they were expecting."

"I know you got him over thirty coupons for his birthday last year…"

"Yeah, but that's not all."

"Oh?" Bailey frowned; she knew her husband could be quite sneaky.

"Well, I hid pacifiers ALL over the house."

"Josh!"

"Carrie told me a couple of weeks ago they're still finding them…"

"JOSHUA!"

"That's not all…" Joshua couldn't look her in the eyes. "I also filled his car with diapers one Friday night when he was out to dinner with coworkers."

"Oh my…"

"But the worst thing I did was I hired the youth group to follow him around one Saturday and they sang 'We're Having a Baby' every thirty minutes from six a.m. until ten p.m. I even had them come in shifts."

Bailey's mouth dropped and she struggled for words. "… You… YOU… Joshua James Cabot, you deserve what you get."

Head hanging down, Joshua muttered, "How long do you think we can hide this pregnancy?"

"I'm not HIDING our baby!"

"Yes, well…"

Bailey sat up and put her hands on the side of Joshua's face. "Sweetheart, this is what we call love for better or worse. Aiden's going to make you pay, but I'll just tell him to leave me out of it. You'll have to suffer through like a big boy."

Chuckling, she turned out the lights. "You've brought this on yourself."

Rolling over, she drifted off, but not before she heard her husband whisper, "We're having a baby!"

About the Author

Anna Christine Boulier has been a writer and storyteller since she begged her mother to learn to read before she entered first grade- to the bane of her first-grade teacher. Since then she has written short stories and had characters that lived in her head for years. In May of 2013, God gave her a story and she wrote it in six weeks. Once the first book lived on paper she couldn't stop. She currently has four books published with more on the way.

She grew up in Cartersville and except for a brief stint in Atlanta for college, she's been there ever since. If you meet her, she can tell you more, because it's a story! Writing is not full time, she pays the bills with a job that helps her stay creative.

**Writing is my testimony- Grace my story!
It isn't just a tagline, but a way of life.**

Made in the USA
Coppell, TX
05 March 2021